THE FATE OF ELEONOR

THE FATE OF ELEONOR

For information contact books@asturianhouse.com

Asturian House Press Ltd., 8300 FM 1960 West, Suite 450, Houston, Texas 77070

ISBN 978-1-959705-01-7 (Paperback)

ISBN 978-1-959705-00-0 (ebook)

Library of Congress Control Number: 2022949236

Cover design by Rena Violet

ASTURIAN
HOUSE PRESS

E.B. BORBÓN

THE FATE OF ELEONOR

ASTURIAN
HOUSE PRESS

CHAPTER ONE

For any lesser being, fleeing through a forest in the middle of the night might pose an issue, but Eleonor had trodden these trails endlessly and knew them more intimately than many knew their lovers. She could run the worn paths around their manor with her eyes closed.

She didn't need to—the flames slowly eating away at her home lit the night sky so even their pursuers with human eyesight could see as if it was daytime. Eleonor could feel the heat from the flames at her back, pushing her forward, reminding her the blaze could have been her fate if she had been just a moment slower in fleeing. Max was right ahead of her, and she wondered if he, too, felt the heat of their lives going up in flames.

An arrow shot past them, whistling as it cut through the air. Eleonor flinched, imagining the pain an arrow tip would cause. Getting hit wouldn't kill her, but it would hurt. If her heart still beat, it would have been jumping out of her chest with adrenaline. She had never fled for her life before, and so far, she didn't care for it.

They had been so careful. She and Max never hunted around

their manor, and in all other ways, they kept to themselves. The isolation was exactly why they had chosen this particular location. It was away from prying eyes, and they could keep to themselves. That was all Eleonor wanted—a quiet life with the man she loved. She deserved that small happiness despite being a vampire, didn't she? They lived righteous lives, well, as righteous as possible given their peculiarity.

So, what had happened? Who had tipped off the hunters? No answer presented itself, and all she could do was run faster. The hunters were falling behind, and if she and Max kept the same pace, they would be able to flee to the safety of the Coven. There was safety in numbers, and she knew the Coven had enough vampires to push back against the hunters.

Skidding into a clearing, she felt relief wash through her. There was another vampire watching them. He was backlit by the moonlight, but she recognized him instantly. "Father," she gasped. She fell still, waiting for his acknowledgment. He was here to help her. They were safe.

"We have to go, Eleonor," Max begged, pulling on her hand to keep her moving.

The relief she felt at finding her father washed away all sense of urgency. Everything would be okay now. They had help. They had her father.

"Eleonor," Max hissed, pulling at her hand. She didn't understand how Max couldn't see how fortunate they had been to run into her father at this moment. "The hunters will be here any second. If you want to get away, we need to go now. They're closing in on us."

"Help us, Father," she implored again.

Her father laughed, high and cold. It made the hair at the back of her neck rise, and her smile slipped from her lips. "I would never help a traitor." He whistled, high and clear, and it took only a second for Eleonor to realize her father was summoning the very hunters they fled.

Max jerked her arm and she stumbled before she found her footing. She had only gone a step when an arrow whizzed past her and into Max's chest. It wasn't enough to kill him, but their aim had been true, and it had pierced his heart. He crumpled to the ground, unable to move.

Once again, she sought out her father, still having trouble reconciling what he'd just done. He had stepped out of the moonlight that filled the clearing, and for the first time, she saw the outlines of others dispersed through the tree line. Her Coven. They were all standing there watching her, waiting.

With an icy certainty, Eleonor realized they'd been betrayed. Their Coven must have tipped off the hunters and made some kind of deal. That was the only reason they weren't helping her. On any other day, the hunters and vampires would fight on sight. This was different. Her heart rebelled at the idea; these vampires were her family.

There was only one reason for them to tip off the hunters—they wanted Eleonor and Max dead. Vampires couldn't directly kill each other, but nothing stopped them from indirectly picking each other off. Never in her wildest dreams had she thought the people who raised her would send her to her grave.

It was her moment of disorientation that did her in. She felt a sharp pain flare in her chest and glanced down to find an arrow sticking out of it. Crumpling to the ground next to Max, Eleonor focused on her body. She could still twitch her fingers, however slight the movement was. The arrow must have only nicked her heart. If it had landed true, she would have been immobile. The ground was cold beneath her and a fallen branch bit into her cheek.

Her eyes didn't seem to be affected, and she sought Max. Although she could still feel his presence, he was out of her field of vision. What she did see was the group of hunters surrounding them, lifting first Max and then herself onto the backs of horses. In the short moments she'd been moving, she saw the Coven members still standing there, watching. The depth of their anger or hatred toward her and Max must have been staggering. Eleonor wondered what she'd done to have her father turn his back on her. Worse, she had the sinking feeling he'd been the one to contact the hunters. It had to have been him, or at the very least, he'd given his permission for someone to do so.

The betrayal cut deeper than she thought possible. She had been turned as a child, and her father was the only parental figure she remembered.

Besides the bouncing ground, Eleonor couldn't see much. They'd put her on her stomach, and the only direction she could see was down. After what felt like a lifetime, the horses stopped and she was thrown into a carriage, if one could call the box on wheels that. The door was shut tight, and Eleonor heard a chain rattle into place. The hunters weren't taking any chances.

The glorified cart jostled them as it carried them away, and she used the motion of the cart to roll toward Max. Using every bit of strength she had, she forced her arm up and laid her hand on his cheek. If these were her final moments, she wanted to be as close to Max as possible.

She ached as she gazed into his eyes. They were full of love and regret and a resignation to his own demise that shook her to her core. He didn't believe they would make it out of this alive, and that knowledge scared her. He'd always been the optimistic one.

"Run," he whispered, barely loud enough for Eleonor to hear. It was a prayer as much as it was a request.

"I can't leave you," Eleonor whispered. A life spent without Max would be worse than death. He was her better half and she'd be lost without him. They'd spent the last two hundred and five years together. How could she carry on without his love?

She wouldn't leave him behind. She'd rather die next to him.

"Run," he repeated again, the desperation in his voice so vivid she could almost taste it. "Promise me."

Eleonor realized this one request was his dying wish. He didn't believe they would survive, but he would do anything in his power to make sure she made it out. How could she deny him this, even if it meant she lost everything?

Her love and respect for him won out. Almost imperceptibly, she nodded. The movement was just enough for Max to see and no more.

Relief clouded his eyes, and Eleonor resolved to run if the opportunity presented itself. She wouldn't look back, even if it meant leaving Max behind. The idea sickened her, but she couldn't deny Max anything, even this.

The rest of the ride was silent, neither of the captured vampires wasting their breath. They conveyed all they needed to say to each other in the gentle looks they exchanged.

The carriage had barely stopped when the doors were flung open. Eleonor hadn't even realized they'd stopped moving, she'd been so focused on remaining calm for Max. She didn't want their last moments together to be filled with panic and helplessness.

Through the open door, she saw a towering pyre. It was massive, and more wood was being added as she watched. It was large enough to burn several victims, but she knew tonight it would only be two.

Max managed a few words through clenched teeth. "Hope dies last, my love. Run. Like you promised."

Rough hands pushed Eleonor aside and the hunters grabbed Max with no regard for his comfort. They pulled him out of the carriage and dragged him to the base of the pyre, where they dropped him unceremoniously on the ground.

Anger coursed through her, but her body was still stuck. The only way to escape like Max wanted was to remove the arrow still embedded in her chest, but that was easier said than done.

Her face was turned toward the chaos, and she watched the first blow land on Max's face, a sickening crunch making its way over to her. At the very least, they'd broken his nose.

Fury coursed through her, giving her the push she needed to start inching her hand toward the shaft of the arrow.

While she was momentarily distracted, a group had formed around Max. Her view was blocked by several hunters' bodies, but she could hear each blow as it landed. Neither Max nor Eleonor could do anything to save him, and that was a bitterness she had never tasted before.

Desperation filled her as one of the hunters drew a sword. She had half convinced herself that if she could just remove the arrow, she could save them both.

"Let the vampire whore see her lover," someone commanded, and the crowd parted to allow Eleonor a clear view of her beloved. She had mere seconds to save him. Her hand had gripped the shaft lightly when the sword swung down, separating Max's head from his body.

Eleonor screamed, but no one heard her over the cheers and the roar of the fire. She wrenched the arrow free, but she was too late. His body and head were already on the pyre, where they were engulfed in flames. Max was gone.

One of the men turned back toward the carriage, ready to do the same to her.

She snarled and leapt out of the carriage, catching the man by surprise. He screamed, raising the alarm, but he was too late to save himself. With her strength fully restored, Eleonor was at the advantage, and she wasted no time in removing his head from his shoulders.

For one single moment, she envisioned seeking her revenge on the people who had destroyed her life. But reason snuck in, and she decided against it. There were too many of them, and besides, Max had told her to flee. Turning, she ran from the village square, dodging between houses until she was back in the woods. She ran away from the village and its residents, away from her home, and most importantly, away from the Coven that had betrayed them and sentenced Max to death.

She ran until an exposed root tripped her, sending her sprawling across the hard ground. She couldn't move another muscle. She knew she was miles from the site of her nightmare, but the urge to go farther remained. She still felt the gazes of the Coven on her back, watching her and Max be taken away.

Silent tears leaked from her eyes, and Eleonor finally allowed herself to cry and mourn the loss of everything. Of Max. With the realization she had nothing left, she cried harder.

CHAPTER TWO

The fluorescent bulb flickered again, and Ellie nearly banged her head against the table in frustration. Having lived through several iterations of lighting, she had to admit that fluorescents were her least favorite. They always flickered, no matter what one did. It was bloody annoying and, to her sensitive eyes, irritating.

She was as annoyed with the lights as she was with the book that lay open before her. It had promised to be a complete compilation of all things vampire related, but really it was nothing more than a ton of myths wrapped up in complete lies. For goodness sake, a cross wasn't going to stop her unless she was impaled with it, and even then, depending on where she was stabbed, she'd be more annoyed than anything. Contrary to popular belief, stabbing someone in the heart was more difficult than one would think.

Placing the book aside, Eleonor groaned. "This is a shitty collection. It doesn't even know fact from fiction. I swear, what a disgrace." She shook her head and picked up the next book in her 'to be read' pile. There was a note attached, dating the book to the 1600s, which instantly increased her curiosity.

Eleonor's excitement died almost as soon as her fingers met the pages. They weren't the right texture for the time period and the ink smelled wrong. It was as if whoever had crafted the shabby counterfeit hadn't even tried. Really, if someone was going to put the effort into a counterfeit, the least they could do was make it a good one. She threw it aside with more force than necessary. The solid thud it made when it landed made her feel better.

"My opinion of your collection is rapidly going downhill. Did you really waste money on this crap? That last one was only a couple of decades old. A novice should have been able to tell you that. Really, you could have hired me, and I would have sorted through all this junk."

Grabbing the last book in her stack, Eleonor tried to bite back her excitement. Finally, something that looked promising. It wasn't as old as she liked—it was only from the 1800s—but she had a good feeling about it. At the very least, the book was authentic. Either that, or it was an uncommonly good forgery.

Throughout the early years of this century, a plague of vampire-caused deaths pervaded the town. Characterized by dual puncture wounds to the neck, the killer left no other calling card, however, a strange woman of Spanish descent was often seen near the murder scenes.

Initially, the town believed the deaths of various criminals to be unrelated, simply judgment from God. It was only after six bodies were found that the bite marks were noted and taken as evidence. This region hadn't seen a vampire death in generations, so the authorities didn't know what to look for.

The Church held a cleansing of the town and the deaths stopped for a short while before picking up with a vengeance. Over a year later, the last death was recorded in the town registrar. As silently as the vampire invaded the village, they slipped away with no repercussions for their actions.

SHE SHUT the book with a sigh. It had been accurate. However, she already knew this story. In fact, she had been the vampire terrorizing the town in question—although killing criminals should have been seen as a favor, really. There had been some terrible men she'd taken care of, and she knew more than one wife hadn't mourned their abusive husbands as diligently as they should.

Since the moment Max left this earth, she had been alone in a way few could imagine. Making her way through Europe and then the New World, she'd hunted alone, choosing to only feed on killers and criminals. Despite her long time on earth, she couldn't feed off the innocent. She didn't have it in her. She chuckled at the idea that she still had some morals, no matter how corrupt. Maybe she wasn't as lost of a cause as she felt, but she counted her discretion more as common decency than any morality she might possess.

She tossed aside the book, and it landed with a softer thump than the previous one. Turning to address the corpse that had once owned the books, she said, "You really had a dismal collection. For someone of your acclaim, I expected better. What were you doing with all your funds? Buying absolute trash?"

The corpse did not respond. Ellie sighed. She really must be losing it, talking to her very dead victim and half expecting a reply. Loneliness was getting to her. That was the only answer.

With a critical eye, Ellie inspected the body. If one didn't know what to look for, the two puncture wounds on his neck would go unnoticed. She had always been a neat feeder and there wasn't a single drop of blood anywhere. It was easier to eat neatly than try to get blood out of her clothing. She had learned that lesson when she first turned.

Usually careful with her selection of meals, she'd gone out on a limb with this guy. After watching him interact with one of his college students, Eleonor had gotten a predatory vibe from the professor. The way he'd eyed his student as if she was a piece of meat had made Ellie's skin crawl. Her suspicions had been confirmed when she bit him.

Like all vampires, Eleonor was privy to a victim's memory when she drank their blood. It wasn't a long glimpse, and she had no control over it, but the memories often gave insight into who the person was or had been. In the professor's case, she'd gotten a glimpse into how he saw his female students, and it had revolted her. She had definitely saved some young woman from his manipulative grasp. Ellie wasn't a good person. She didn't think she was a bad person either, but no one would call her a hero. However, she'd learned long ago that there were people who were just bad out there, her current victim included. Sometimes it really was that cut and dry.

Rising, she inspected the rest of the room. On the surface, his collection seemed impressive, but after closer inspection, Ellie realized over half the items were fakes. For someone who was supposed to be an expert, he sure sucked at choosing books and artifacts.

Going back to his desk, Ellie plopped back into the chair and stared at the corpse on the other side of the room. Dead bodies didn't bother her anymore. When she was younger, they had terrified her—she'd been convinced the corpses would reanimate and attack her, seeking their revenge for their deaths. Now, it would only be an interesting pastime to deal with a reanimated corpse.

She bit back a chuckle. After all, wasn't she just a reanimated corpse with good self-control? She didn't even have a soul to differentiate herself from the man on the floor. Really, they were more alike than different. Whatever souls they may have had were long gone.

Ellie went over and grabbed the book she'd tossed onto his chest. A bubble of amusement forced a thin smile onto her lips. She rarely smiled anymore—there wasn't anything to smile about, but this book had entertained her, if only for a moment.

As she flipped through the pages, random words and phrases popped out at her. On some level, she was impressed there had been enough of her exploits to fill an entire book. On another, she guessed living with her affliction for so long meant her exploits could fill hundreds of books. At one time, she'd reveled in the new and exciting, but not anymore. She hadn't enjoyed living for hundreds of years, if she could call what she did living. Was someone living if their heart didn't beat anymore?

She shut the book and dropped it again. Something about killing put her in a philosophical mood. It always had, even when she was much younger. Max used to tease her about it when she posed impossible questions not meant to have answers. She'd always loved stumping him, which was rare. He was brilliant and had always been in his alchemy lab doing one thing or another. Much of what he did had gone over her head, but what she did understand had always been fascinating. Nowadays, he'd be called a nerd, but back then, she had been mesmerized by his passion.

She still missed him every day. Whoever said time healed all wounds was wrong, and she envied those who were able to heal at all. No matter how much time had passed, her wound was still gaping, and she felt Max's absence keenly. Sometimes when she woke from her daytime slumber, she still rolled over to search for his body next to hers. Those evenings were particularly difficult for her to weather.

It occurred to her suddenly that the corpse might have a family. Looking around, she saw no pictures or personal touches in the office. She guessed when he was trying to seduce students, he didn't want pictures of his family watching. Taking a quick look at his left hand, she found no wedding ring. Good.

Her mind wandered back to the matter of souls, and she wondered where her victim's soul had gone. She wasn't convinced there even was anything beyond this world, but if there was, she hoped he was being punished for his lecherous actions.

It was a shame she'd never find out. Even if she was killed, it was a universally accepted fact that vampires didn't have souls. Whatever happened when their bodies transformed and their bodies died killed their souls, too.

Glancing at the clock, she realized she had stayed far longer than she intended. It was almost two in the morning. At some point, she had to leave if she didn't want to be caught.

Taking one last look around, she paused when her eyes landed on the corpse. "Your collection is terrible."

She turned and made her way out of the office, leaving the door slightly ajar for the rats. Pausing, she sent out a mental call for the New York City rats to visit her friend. Those rats were no joke and would have the body almost picked clean by the time anyone found him. Even if her puncture wounds were found, no one would think anything of them.

It was a breeze leaving the empty community college campus. No other professors or students were around, and the security guard was taking a nap in his chair as she passed. Ellie almost wished for a more challenging escape. Almost.

If she was still human, she'd hesitate to stroll through the streets of New York City alone at this time of night, but she was the scariest monster out there. She'd welcome death if it came for her, but killing a vampire was exceptionally difficult. Sunlight didn't kill them, although it did make them significantly weaker. Even a stake through the heart wouldn't do it. Now, if it was silver coated, a stake through the heart, it would paralyze a vampire, but even that wouldn't kill them. Vampires were very hardy creatures.

No one bothered Ellie as she strolled, and she was almost disappointed. A fight would have been an interesting addition to her night.

Her phone dinged, indicating a new email. There were some vampires who shunned new technology, but she wasn't one of them. Smartphones were convenient for numerous reasons.

Excitement coursed through her as she stared at the subject line. Thoth's Books had just received a new shipment, and the owner had kindly set them aside for her to browse first. Turning around, Ellie headed toward the bookstore. Despite the late hour, it would be open. The store catered to an eccentric clientele and as such, kept nontraditional hours. Maybe she would have better luck there. At this point, it wouldn't take much to be an improvement over the professor's collection.

CHAPTER THREE

The bell above the door jingled a happy tune, letting the owner know he had a client. Walking through the doorway was like walking through an invisible force field; the outside and inside felt different from each other in a noticeable way. For the thousandth time, she wondered if the store was warded. The owner was odd, yes, but he didn't reek of magic the way witches and warlocks did. However, if it was and the wards let through a vampire, she didn't want to think about what they might keep out. Sure, she was a monster that went bump in the night, but there was always something worse out there.

The owner, Mr. Gootu, popped out of nowhere, as was his habit, and surprised her. Somehow, he slipped by her heightened senses every time she visited, and she was almost positive he did it on purpose. "Good, good, you got my message. It's a pleasure to see you again, Ellie." His voice was reedy and had the unfortunate tone of nails on a chalkboard. With his bent back and constant shuffle, he appeared to be elderly, and Ellie might have believed that if she hadn't seen him maneuver through the cluttered shop with ease when no one was looking. She was almost positive his elderly appearance was all an act.

There were too many contradictions with Mr. Gootu, and she always felt a bit nervous around him. Nobody made her nervous, not anymore. She'd thought herself beyond such a feeling until she came across this shop. Standing before Mr. Gootu, she felt as if all her secrets were laid bare, like she was just another open book to him. Perhaps, after all the years in his bookstore, he had become a reader of people as well as books.

"This way, this way," he said, motioning Ellie toward a back room. In all her time coming here, she had only ever been allowed into one of the many back rooms. She wondered what other secrets were held away from prying eyes. Maybe someday she would ask, but not tonight. Tonight, she just wanted to see what had come in.

Entering the small room, she found a table with a partially unpacked box of books sitting on it. At first glance, they appeared to be exactly what Ellie was searching for. Many of the books had peeling covers and loose bindings betraying their age. The older the better, as far as she was concerned. One that had already been pulled out looked like it had dried blood on it. She made a mental note to check that one first.

"You have first dibs on anything you want. I'll post the rest online when you're done making your selection." He smiled at her with more gums than teeth, but it was a genuine expression.

She felt a smile tug at her own lips in reply. "Thank you, Mr. Gootu. I really appreciate it."

With a nod, he hobbled out of the room, leaving Ellie alone. She appreciated he wasn't the type of owner to breathe down her neck as she looked. To be fair, she would never do anything to ruin a book, even if it wasn't what she was looking for. Her years of research had taught her the value of every text, regardless of its content.

Unpacking the rest of the box, she quickly sorted the books

into two piles—ones that were quickly discarded as not important and another stack that indicated they had some potential. Once she had completed her initial sorting, she took the maybe stack and lowered herself to the floor. All she did tended to have a certain gracefulness to it. Max used to say she should be a dancer, but as a vampire, it was an unrealistic goal. There weren't too many midnight performances.

A more in-depth perusal got rid of the first couple of books, but then her eyes landed on a familiar name—Javier Rodriquez. She'd known a Javier Rodriquez once upon a time. Picking up the book, she turned it over in her hands. It couldn't be the same vampire who had often visited her Coven, could it? He had such a common name. This had to be from someone else who wrote about vampires.

With shaking fingers, she opened the book to the first page of writing.

After months of traveling alone, I came across a Coven today in my exploration of the forest. It was recently formed and appeared to still be working out the politics of such an organization, but I have faith in them. They appear to be levelheaded, and no one is suffering from extreme bloodlust, the sickness that makes monsters of us all. In fact, they have a highly developed feeding schedule and rules that must be followed to keep their location secret from humanity and hunters. They live within days' reach of a town, but far enough away that a stray human wouldn't wander into their Coven.

They are highly structured, and the leader, Aurelio, runs a tight ship. The other members of the Coven seem to fear him as much as they respect him, which isn't a bad thing for a Coven Leader. He seems to revel in his position, and I am quite positive he would do anything within his power to stay Coven Leader. I would prefer not to get on his bad side.

They were happy to have me, and I was even more pleased to be among my own kind after such a long time traveling alone. Although I am often in the company of humans, the comfort of not having to hide what I am was palpable. It's like finally being able to breathe after being suffocated, but not noticing at the time you were struggling.

SHE GAZED down at the book, stunned. It was the Javier she'd known. At some point, he must have taken his journals he was always writing in and published them as fiction. Flipping to the front, she scanned to see what the date of publication was, but it gave no hints. By virtue of the paper and ink, she guessed it was from the early 1800s.

THE LEADER of the Coven has a young daughter. Well, she's young compared to me. She and her partner are both bright and give me hope for our future as a species. If only we had more like them.

She was a delight to spend time with, and she had so many questions about my travels. I must admit I was flattered by the attention. Her partner was interested in my travels as well, along with what alchemy I'd come across. They really are a delightful pair who love each other deeply.

ELLIE TURNED the page and nearly dropped the book. A portrait of her and Max stared back at her, their eyes alight with laughter. She felt like she had been hit. If she'd been prepared, the shock might have been less, but having it sprung upon her was painful. She had no pictures of Max, only what her mind had held on to over the years.

She traced the gentle curve of Max's cheek, her fingers remembering the feel of his flesh beneath it. Javier had captured Max's light so well she might as well have been looking at a picture, not a sketch.

Turning to her own image, she inspected the girl she'd been. She barely recognized herself. Time had worn her and although she was still uncommonly pretty by human standards, the joy she'd once felt for life had dimmed until it had died away, and it showed on her face.

The smiling woman in the sketch was as dead as Max. That smile, filled with joy, never graced her lips anymore. It was gone, a piece of the vampire she no longer was. Her lips didn't even curl up at the edges anymore.

"Excuse me," a voice said behind her, making her jump. Humans—minus Mr. Gootu, if he was human—rarely were capable of sneaking up on her, and she'd had no clue she wasn't alone in the room anymore.

Ellie turned and found a man standing behind her and slightly to the right. He had light brown wavy hair that looked as if he'd run his hands through it several times, leaving it almost wild but still appealing even to her immortal eye. She was still sitting down, yet she could tell he was at least six inches taller than her. She felt almost small beside him.

"I see you've found a copy of *The Story*. I was just researching it online. Did you know it was the first instance of vampires being introduced into literature? It's a shame it's not more well known." His voice was on the softer side, but Ellie guessed that had more to do with the environment than anything else. He'd had the confidence to walk up to a complete stranger and interrupt them, so he couldn't be shy.

"That's interesting," Ellie hedged. It wasn't a lie; she was intrigued by the book—journal, whatever it was—even if the reasoning was very different.

"May I see it?" he asked.

She hesitated for just a moment before nodding and handing over the book. He took it with gentle hands.

"I've already decided to buy it," she blurted out, noticing how his eyes lit up when he grabbed it.

"Oh." He sighed and handed the book back to her. "Then you should take this back before I get too excited. It would make a fine addition to my extensive collection." After a pause, he asked, "Are you a historian?"

"I'm more of an...expert." If living through history made someone an expert, she definitely was one of the best. Technically speaking, she'd lived through more history than any human alive ever would. Vampires had long memories, and hers was excellent, which was both a blessing and a curse. There were many things she would rather forget.

Ellie hesitated, not sure what else to say. Small talk wasn't really her thing, especially with humans. She had long ago given up on trying to relate to anyone.

"That's excellent!" the man said. "Do you want to get coffee tomorrow? I'd love to pick your brain and hear about your collection." After a moment, he stuck out his hand. "I'm Julian, by the way."

She blinked up at him. He'd rushed through his speech, and her brain needed a moment to catch up. Rising, she took his hand. "Ellie. Ellie Leon." The fake name never felt natural on her tongue even though she'd been going by it for years. Eleonor de León was dead, or as dead as she could be.

Julian didn't seem to notice and smiled at her, warm and open. She could tell he had no secrets and she wondered for a moment what that would be like. What a life he must lead, free to do as he wanted. A life out of the shadows that cloaked her.

"We should meet for coffee tomorrow at The Brew. Does this time work for you? I'd love to pick your brain." He smiled again.

She opened her mouth to decline the invitation but found herself saying instead, "Sure. I'd like that." If he had books that could help her, she owed it to herself and Max.

In addition, there was something that piqued her interest about Julian. Sure, he was attractive, but it was more than that.

There were lots of attractive men around who would be more than happy to entertain Ellie. None of them had ever caught her attention before.

No, there was something different about Julian. She just couldn't put her finger on what it was. Realizing she was interested in a living being other than herself shocked her, no matter how small her curiosity was.

"I'd better get going," he said, giving the book in her hands one last longing glance. If it hadn't had her portrait with Max in it, she might have considered letting Julian have the book, his look was so pathetic. Instead, she nodded and watched him walk away empty-handed before turning back to the rest of the books.

CHAPTER FOUR

On her approach to the coffee shop the next night, Ellie could see Julian sitting in the window waiting for her. The interior lights backlit him and she wondered again why she'd agreed to come. It was very out of character for her. She kept to herself and avoided anyone she could. Other vampires weren't safe, and humanity was like ants —everywhere and inconsequential.

She almost turned and walked away, but Julian saw her and waved through the window. She guessed that was her sign to stay and have coffee with him. An hour couldn't hurt, right? She could do an hour, then make her excuses and leave, never to see him again. That wouldn't be so bad.

For the hundredth time, she wondered why Julian had approached her. Was it really just because of that book? Or had he had another reason? For half a second, she considered the possibility he was a hunter, but she quickly dismissed the idea. In truth, she wouldn't be upset if a hunter came after her; she'd finally have her out. But nothing about Julian had given her the impression he hunted monsters.

Pushing open the coffee shop door, she flinched at the sound the bell made. It was loud and harsh, not at all like the bookstore's pleasant jingle. She made her way over to Julian and set her bag down.

"Do you want coffee or something else?" Julian asked.

Ellie was about to decline the offer when she thought better of it. Having a mug would give her something to do with her hands. She didn't need to eat or drink human food, but she hadn't lost the ability to. It was just less pleasant than it used to be. It was as if all the flavors were muted and unless highly seasoned, most food tasted flat.

Julian passed her a ten-dollar bill from his wallet. "My treat."

Ellie nodded and grabbed the money without comment. When she got to the counter, she debated briefly between a latte and a tea, ultimately deciding a jasmine tea sounded delicious. She waited while the barista made it and when she held her steaming mug, she made her way back to the table where Julian waited.

Handing him his change, she said, "Thank you for the tea."

"No problem." He rose as she sat, and once she'd claimed her seat, he sat back down.

When he smiled at her, Ellie realized his smile was easily given. He probably smiled at strangers when he passed them on the street. What a curious thought. Ellie mostly kept her head down and was grateful small talk wasn't common between strangers in New York, unlike when she'd traveled the South. That had been a painful experience.

An awkward silence stretched between them, and Ellie had to remind herself once again why she was there. He had offered her a partnership that had the potential to work wonders for her. She had spent a pretty penny on the book last night, but she didn't regret purchasing it. She was even willing to loan it to Julian if he had a good collection and allowed her to look at his books.

There was one book she had been hunting for years. *The*

Vampire Hunter's Handbook. Every once in a while, she'd heard a rumor that a copy had been located, but she'd never been able to lay her hands on one, which was weird considering the book had been translated into multiple languages, many of which she spoke. After traveling all over Europe and the Americas, she had picked up quite a few languages. Languages were something she learned easily, which had helped her throughout her long life. Despite this, there was still some slang she didn't understand. She guessed that was just part of staying away from people.

A Latin version of the book had gone up for sale just last year on eBay. She'd thought she had finally found a break, but the listing was taken down before she'd been able to bid on it. Part of her felt like there was some cosmic interference preventing her from laying hands on the book, but she wasn't sure she believed in a higher power. Maybe once she had, but not anymore.

Regardless of price, if a copy crossed her path, she would buy it. As far as she was aware, it was the only book in existence that listed tried and true methods to kill a vampire. She needed that book. After years of consideration, she had come to the decision that if she ever found the book, she would use it to either kill herself or to seek revenge on the Coven that had betrayed her. She didn't know which was her preference; she changed her mind often on the topic. Some days all she wanted was to die, and other days, revenge was her focus. When she first started looking for the book, she'd decided she would make that decision when she had to.

Maybe it was just wishful thinking caused by loneliness and grief, but there was something of Max in Julian's calm mannerisms. For instance, he had risen just as Max had the first time they'd met, allowing her to sit before he sat again. Despite the oddity of their current situation, he appeared perfectly calm and composed sitting across from her. Ellie, on the other hand, had to fight the urge to fidget. She had never been one to sit still for long.

At that first meeting, Max had been so handsome with his dark-blond hair ruffled by the wind, towering over her. Ellie had been smitten with the handsome Englishman. He'd spoken perfect Spanish to her at their greeting, and she'd almost swooned. Of course, not even an hour after their first meeting, they'd been sparring on the training field. They'd both wanted to be Coven guards and the training was intense. She still remembered his surprise when she'd brought him to his knees, some of his arrogance gone.

The memory was bittersweet, and she twisted her lips at its taste.

"Something wrong?" Julian asked, concern lacing his words.

"No," Ellie said, clearing her face of all expression. "I was just thinking." It had been a long time since she had spoken at length with a living human, and she hoped she wasn't being too awkward. "What do you do?" she asked, trying to turn the conversation to safer topics.

Julian brightened. "I'm working on my PhD in history. I only have a year left before I graduate, but it seems like time is going exceptionally slow."

She raised an eyebrow. "That must be fascinating."

"It is," he agreed. A light pink tinged his cheeks. "Truth be told, this is my second PhD. I already have one in chemistry."

"Wow," Ellie said. She was impressed despite herself. She had always been smart, but she'd been a terrible student. If it hadn't interested her, she couldn't make herself care about it. It had always been one of her failings, whereas Max had been a sponge able to soak up any and all knowledge. "What made you go back for your second one? I would think getting one PhD would be enough for most people."

"Don't laugh at me," he said, grinning. "My ultimate goal is to get funding to recreate alchemical experiments."

Ellie stared at him, surprised. "Why do you want to do that?"

"I've always been fascinated by alchemy, and I really believe some of the experiments are valid and yielded results. I just need the money and space to prove it. That's where my PhDs come in. They give me the credibility I need to secure funds."

"What made you interested in alchemy?"

Julian's eyes lit up, and she could tell he was passionate about the topic. "When I was eight or nine, I found an old book in my grandfather's study about alchemy. When I asked him about it, he told me I could have it. It was fascinating, and after that, I was hooked. I've been collecting books on it ever since, both instruction guides and general stories about it. Thoth's Books has been a godsend. I don't know where he finds his books, but I'm not going to question it."

"Do you still have it?" she asked.

"Have what?"

"The book your grandfather gave you."

He smiled. "I do. It's not worth much, but it's one of my favorites just the same. Besides being an interesting read, it reminds me of my grandfather. He's been gone a couple years now, but every time I pick up that book, it's as if he just left the room."

There was no reason for his answer to touch her, but she still felt the flutter of something in her chest. She wasn't used to feeling anything anymore and couldn't place exactly what she felt.

"Have you done any experiments from any of the books you've collected?" Ellie asked, finding she was genuinely interested in his answer. Max had always been experimenting, and some of the results had been wondrous.

"When I was a kid, I experimented all the time. It drove my mother mad, all the mess I made, but my dad was just happy I was enjoying myself. I was an only kid and I think he feared I might be lonely." The soft smile on his face betrayed his feelings for his parents.

She didn't remember her birth parents, and she tried not to think of her adoptive father. Even after all this time, the anger and betrayal she felt toward him was still too fresh.

"What about you? How'd you start collecting?" Julian asked.

She shrugged. "Morbid curiosity about vampires, I guess. Personally, I find them far more interesting than werewolves or witches. It's probably the blood thing." After a moment's pause, she asked, "You think it's real—alchemy, I mean, don't you?"

Without hesitation, he nodded. "I do."

Ellie nodded back. She knew how real it was—Max had been a dedicated practitioner. He had devoted innumerable hours to his laboratory.

"I know I sound crazy, but there's a certain logic to the work that had to yield results. It's like math or science—there's a self-regulating component that just makes sense in most experiments."

"What would you do, if you proved alchemy was real?" she asked.

He tilted his head, mulling over her question. "There's the fun alchemy stuff, like turning other metals into gold, but I have books filled with recipes that are supposed to create cures and help people. Those are the ones I'm most interested in recreating. I mean, an endless supply of gold sounds nice, but alchemy offers so much more than that."

Ellie had to admit she was pleased with his answer. It showed a depth of character she respected.

"You must think I'm insane." He laughed, avoiding her gaze.

"No, I think you're right." She graced him with a real smile. It felt forced, but he didn't seem to notice and smiled back at her.

She had come to a decision—she would help Julian so she could have access to his books. Even if he didn't have the book she was looking for, she knew there were alchemy solutions that affected vampires. Once, she'd known a little bit about them, but that had been years ago, and she had never committed them to memory. Maybe she would be able to find a recipe for him and convince Julian to make it for her. Maybe she would find a peaceful exit from this world.

"I'd be happy to trade knowledge with you." This time her smile was more genuine, and Julian lit up, delighted.

"Wonderful. Let's start tomorrow."

CHAPTER FIVE

The second time they met was as awkward for Ellie as the first, but after several late-night sessions where they pored over texts, she was feeling more comfortable with Julian. Apparently, socializing was easier if one did it often, and by their third meeting, Julian had even managed to make her laugh. The sound was like tinkling glass, and it had surprised her that it still sounded so pleasant after all the years she hadn't used it. Julian had been as surprised as she was that she'd laughed, but he'd worn a pleased smile on his face the rest of the night.

"I have a suggestion," Julian said at their sixth meeting, pulling out the third book from his bag. Ellie marveled at how he had fit all the books in such a small backpack. Hers was at least twice his in size, yet she had only been able to pack four books safely.

"Mhm?" she hummed, already diving into the first book he'd produced. It mentioned vampires in the title, and she hoped it was more about vampires than alchemy.

"Why don't we just go to my house? Then I won't have to lug

all these books around. My back is killing me. I also have more than just coffee or tea." He motioned toward the jasmine tea that had become her go-to when they were at the coffee shop.

Ellie glanced up at him, surprised. They had been using the coffee shop up until this point, and although it was rarely busy at two in the morning, there were still a few dedicated caffeine addicts populating the tables around them. She was about to open her mouth and decline when she realized his house would offer more privacy than the coffee shop. They weren't doing anything illegal, but it still felt illicit, perhaps because she was hiding her true intentions from him. Then again, maybe she just wasn't used to being out and about in society, even if it was just the late-night crowd.

She hesitated for just a moment before nodding. "Sure. Do you want to go there now, or should we wait until next time?" She wasn't sure which scenario was better, and she was happy to defer to him.

Julian cocked his head. It hadn't taken her long to realize he did this when he was considering something seriously. "Why don't we go now? It's only a twenty-minute walk from here, if you're up for that." He looked at the large stack of books she had pulled out of her own bag. "Can you walk that far lugging all that?"

"That's fine. I'll be fine." She started packing up, and within five minutes, they were on their way to Julian's place.

"I swear I'm not a serial killer," he blurted out as they walked, waving his hands in the air for emphasis.

She turned to him, surprised. "I didn't think you were. What made you say that?"

He blushed, and despite herself, Ellie found it endearing. He looked so young when he did it, she could picture him as a boy perfectly. His mother must have had a hard time staying mad at him when he was in trouble. Ellie knew she would have. "I just

—well—I just convinced you to come to my house alone at two in the morning. I wanted you to know I didn't have anything nefarious planned."

Ellie laughed softly. "I don't think you have any ill intentions." Besides, in a fight, Ellie would win, hands down. Julian might have a toned body, but Ellie was stronger and faster than any human. "Even if you did, I think I could take you."

Julian raised an eyebrow as he looked down at her but didn't comment on their obvious size difference. "Why are you always up at night?" he finally asked.

Surprised by the question, Ellie hesitated before saying, "I guess at this point, I'm nocturnal. I find I sleep best during the day, which means I'm up at night. What about you? You're meeting me at two in the morning. Don't you have classes during the day?"

Julian sighed. "My sleep schedule is all messed up. I'm up most nights anyways, so I don't have a problem meeting at this time."

"Do you ever fall asleep during class?"

With a grimace, Julian nodded. "It's been known to happen. Luckily my professors are good sports about it, although I did wake up in one of my classes with a bunch of question marks drawn on my face. Took me over an hour to figure out why everyone was giggling. They said it was because I'd have a bunch of questions about what I'd missed."

Ellie tried to keep her smile from spreading on her face and coughed into her hand to hide it.

As they walked, neither Ellie nor Julian felt the need to fill the silence with meaningless chatter. There was a companionship between them that filled in any cracks, and for the duration of their walk, Ellie allowed herself to feel, if not happy, then not sad. She didn't know Julian very well, but she did know she was relieved not to be completely alone again. If her days weren't brighter, then they definitely weren't as dark as they used to be. Walking with someone was nice, even if it was just with a human. Maybe she should get a cat. A dog was too much work, but a cat would be great company.

They reached the small brownstone Julian owned, and he unlocked the door with a great deal of shaking. "It's the lock," he explained as he finally got the door open.

She nodded, as if that made any sense at all, and entered. Instantly, she was hit with a sense of home. Home wasn't something one could make happen—it occurred naturally in a well-loved well-used space, and Julian's place had it.

Her apartment was in the basement of her building and her landlord was shady at best, but he accepted cash and left her alone and that was all she needed. There had been rats there when she moved in, but after politely willing them to leave, she'd had no problems with them.

"I have a whole room dedicated to my books," he said. "It's even temperature controlled. I splurged a bit on it, I have to admit." After leading her upstairs, he opened the first door on the left with a flourish. He was excited to show her his collection and Ellie thought it was cute.

Ellie entered and was a bit shocked by how many books filled the room. It was bigger than she'd expected, and she realized he must have turned the master bedroom into this mini library. A man after her own heart, although his was beating and hers was not.

The smell of old paper and old ink permeated the room, and she breathed it in like a rare perfume. "Wow." If Julian didn't have her book, he probably had a dozen others that might help her.

Julian smirked but didn't say anything, enjoying her obvious appreciation of his collection.

Starting with the books on her left, she began cataloging the collection in her mind, noting the ones she wanted to look at. Before she took anything down, she wanted to have a general idea of what was present. He had quite a few that would be beneficial in her search even though the majority of them were alchemy related.

"You can look at whatever you want, but please use gloves if you take out the ones from the glass case. If you don't mind, I'd like to photocopy some of the pages from one of the books you brought. My copier is in the next room." He reached for the backpack she was still wearing, and she handed it over. A copier wasn't going to damage her books.

"Go ahead," she said.

With boyish delight, he shuffled through the bag until he found the book he wanted. By the time he got back, she'd pulled several tomes from his shelves and had them spread out on the floor. He didn't have a copy of *The Vampire Hunter's Handbook*, but he did have several books written by people she'd known years ago, both human and vampire. It was like the hand of friendship reaching out through time. None of them had portraits of her in them, but she was sure at least one of the books written by vampires mentioned her.

"Found something to keep you interested?" he asked.

She nodded; her eyes still glued to the page she was reading. She was fascinated by the description of her father in the text. Names weren't used, but she had no doubt it was about him.

"You know, I can't really figure out what you're searching for. Your reading selections are all over the place," he mused as he sat down at the small desk shoved into the corner. She didn't answer, and he turned to his copies with a highlighter, not needing a response.

Several hours later, she happened upon an interesting passage in the alchemy book she had picked up.

. . .

After much trial and error, I have developed a draught of endless sleep. The project was modeled after the slumber vampires experience during the day. Contrary to common thought, sunlight does not kill a vampire. In fact, all it does is weaken them. It is like a lizard in the cold—everything about them slows down. However, if one is woken from their slumber, they function purely on instinct, becoming the rabid demons of myth.

The project I've been working on creates an endless sleep for the participant until the sun sets, at which point they rise. There were many complications with the application, as participants slept much too long at first. Over time, this issue was corrected, and at this point, I can assure the safety of the draught.

At the bottom of the page, there was an almost illegible footnote. After turning the book first one way and then the other, she was able to decipher the Latin. *For further explanation on vampire anatomy, consult The Vampire Hunter's Handbook.*

"What is it?" Julian asked, his attention wholly directed at her. She must have made a sound when she realized what the footnote said, betraying her excitement.

"Oh. This book just mentions another book I've been searching for for some time." She prayed he wouldn't ask any more questions, but her prayers went unanswered.

"What book?"

She froze, unsure of what to say. She had already told him she was into vampire stuff, so there wasn't any reason not to tell him, right? What harm could really come from confiding her true goal to him? "I've been searching for a copy of *The Vampire Hunter's Handbook* for several years now. This book"—she pointed to the footnote—"mentions it and it's exciting to receive confirmation that at some point it did exist, even if I can't find it now."

"What do you want that for? Planning to hunt some

vampires?" he teased, not knowing how close to the truth he was.

She forced a chuckle that sounded off to her own ears. "No, nothing like that. I just think the different take on vampires is interesting. Supposedly, there's a translation of the book in every known language going back to the ancient Egyptians. I would love to get my hands on any copy, really, but I'm starting to lose all hope that any copies still exist."

"I've heard of it, although I've never given it much thought. Not really my area of specialty. But I'll keep an eye out for it. I do have some connections, since I'm still in school. And hey, don't give up hope. It dies last."

Hope dies last.

Some of the last words Max had ever said to her.

She cocked her head to the side. "Where did you hear that?"

He blinked innocently. "Hear what?"

"That phrase. Hope dies last."

Julian shrugged. "I don't know, actually. It's something I've always said. I think I heard it from my dad, maybe? He was an eternal optimist. Annoyingly positive, one might say."

An eternal optimist, she thought. *What a refreshing change.*

He smiled over at her, and she smiled back, a real smile this time, one that split her cheeks. His gaze lowered, casting down the length of her body before settling on the pages of the book before them. She felt a stirring deep in her gut—a gentle pull of something familiar she hadn't felt in centuries. It urged her to close the distance between them and feel the heat of his body against the frigid chill of her own. She resisted the pull but marveled at the new sensations. It had been a long time since she enjoyed anyone's company, and an even longer time since someone made her smile in earnest.

Perhaps Max and Julian's father were right. There was always hope, even if there was nothing else.

Max said that before they cut off his head and threw his body to the flames, she thought. *What good did hope do him?*

Ashamed of her feelings, she averted her gaze. She had no right to feel happiness, even for a second. Not when Max was gone from this world.

CHAPTER SIX

Julian ran his hand up her side and over her shoulder to cup the back of her neck. Ellie allowed him to tip her head back, and when their lips met, she gasped. Soft and sure, he captured her lips and angled himself for better access. Ellie groaned in pleasure, enjoying every move of his tongue against hers.

She pushed her body into his, greedy to feel every warm inch of him against her. It had been ages since she'd felt like this. Her body felt alive again, and she was going to savor every second of it.

Max pulled away from her lips and whispered, "My Eleonor," in her ear.

She reared back, confused, panicked. Hadn't it just been Julian kissing her like he needed her tongue in his mouth to breathe? Her head spun and became a disoriented storm of blond curls as Julian's—no, Max's—brow furrowed.

She blinked and shook her head.

Julian tightened his arms around her. His mask of concern remained his own and did not disintegrate into Max's. "Ellie?"

"What's happening?" she whispered. There was a tinge of fear in her voice, and she couldn't disguise it as anything else.

He smiled at her. "Am I that good of a kisser?"

Her senses could not be trusted. Men did not simply change into other men. Her mind was playing tricks on her. Almost three hundred years was a long time to pine after a man, and after not being kissed like this in so long, it only made sense that her instinct would be to concoct a safe image of her first love. Right?

She allowed Julian to kiss her, although she was less swept away than she had been the first time. The thought of Max that was now planted in her head distracted her from the moment. She enjoyed Julian's kiss, but she couldn't help feeling like she was doing something wrong.

Like she was committing a betrayal. No matter how much being in Julian's arms felt like coming home, something felt wrong.

Wracked with confusion, she pulled away and Julian now had half of Max's face, half his own. Their smiles twisted together, and he spoke her name over and over. She scurried away into a darkness that swallowed her whole, but the Julian Max man followed and reached for her. A scholar's soft fingers curled in her hair before the skin became charred and burned, ravaged by flames like Max's corpse had been all those years ago.

She screamed and hurled herself backward, out of his arms and the dream she hadn't realized she'd been having.

Ellie lay in her bed, waiting for the physical effects to dissipate. She was disconcerted to find out that her body had responded to her dream, and she was as aroused as she was confused. More irritated than anything, she pushed aside the arousal, but the confusion lingered.

What had the dream meant? She was a firm believer that dreams were never just dreams. Maybe a long time ago they had been, when she was in love and her Coven still cherished her, but not anymore.

It had been several weeks since Julian had promised to help her find a copy of *The Vampire Hunter's Handbook*, but they'd turned up nothing useful. There had been several mentions of vampires throughout the texts she'd looked at in Julian's collection, but all the information had been based on myth, not fact. Any mention of a stake through the heart was a dead giveaway the author didn't know what they were talking about.

Some of the information was almost laughable.

Vampires were supernaturally hardy creatures. The only ways she knew to kill one was to behead them or incinerate them—or both if you wanted to be certain.

Like what the hunters had done to Max.

Ellie wasn't ashamed to admit that she'd tried to kill herself over the years, with little success. It turned out beheading yourself was harder than she'd thought, despite her creativity and her best efforts.

Eventually, she'd come to the conclusion that burning herself alive was the better, if more painful, option. She'd been proven wrong. She'd flung herself into the flames, or at least she thought she had. It had been quite a shock when she'd woken up in a cave mostly healed from her burns. She held a certain anger that she wasn't even allowed to end her misery when she was paying for someone else's sins.

Directly killing another vampire was nearly impossible to do, including killing herself. Perhaps it was even harder. Too bad she couldn't just drop dead of a broken heart. Her body was literally hardwired to stay alive whether she wanted to be or not. What a disloyal bitch.

Rolling over, she stared at the wall. She didn't have much down here in her basement apartment. The bedroom had only her mattress on the floor and nothing else. Nothing graced the walls aside from the bedsheet that covered the tiny window near the ceiling. There were only three of those throughout the entire apartment, and blocking them had been the first thing she'd done when she'd moved in.

The rest of the basement apartment she rented was the same —empty. Her kitchen didn't even have pots and pans. What was the point? She didn't eat and she had no one else to cook for.

Today was going to be a bad day. She could just feel it. Perhaps it would have been anyway, despite the dream, but the day had definitely started out on a sour note. How could she dream about Julian that way when she still loved Max?

After an hour, she forced herself out of bed and into the shower, where she promptly sat down. Once upon a time, she'd heard that people who were depressed were more likely to sit while showering. Ellie didn't know if that was an actual fact, but she still agreed with it. She was the poster child of tortured and traumatized, after all.

The water ran cold before she picked herself up off the floor. The frigid spray felt good against her cold flesh, but she couldn't stay here forever.

She tried not to think, which was easier said than done. Concentrating on keeping her mind perfectly blank, she washed her hair. She'd kept it long her entire existence, and when dry, it fell down in waves. She'd never seriously considered cutting it, but there were moments when she was so fed up with it, she entertained the idea for a brief moment. Maybe she would look good with short hair. Wasn't that what the humans did after a bad heartbreak? Chopped their hair or dyed it some new, outlandish color? She supposed such impulse decisions happened immediately after said heartbreak, not three hundred years later.

Her body didn't scar, and as she washed it, she wondered what stories would be told by her flesh if she did. Scars were roadmaps to the past, and looking at her, one would think she had none.

Stepping out of the shower, Ellie grabbed a towel. After wrapping herself up, she stared at her reflection. It was another myth that vampires couldn't see their reflections. When mirrors were still made with a silver backing, there'd been some distortion of the reflection but not anymore. It was rare to come across a silver-backed mirror. The cheap one in her bathroom wasn't one, so she could see her reflection perfectly.

Sadness oozed from her pores, the kind that ended lives and destroyed others. Physically, she was perfect, but her eyes told a different story. Whoever had said eyes were the windows to the soul hadn't been lying.

Poets and broken souls, she thought.

For a moment, she wondered what Julian saw when he looked at her. Had he spoken to her in the bookstore because he didn't see the depths of pain in her eyes, or because he *had* seen it and wanted to save her from herself? She pushed away the thought. She didn't need to feel worse than she already did. Thoughts of Julian were off-limits.

Turning away from the mirror in disgust, Ellie quickly got dressed in sweatpants and a t-shirt. Over the years, she'd learned to appreciate the more comfortable clothing society had to offer. She still owned a few nice things for special occasions, but those were few and far between. Her life didn't really involve grand events anymore. Besides, dressing like humans helped her fit in.

She considered leaving her apartment and walking around the city. The sun had already set, and the night posed no danger to her. After a moment's consideration, she decided she wasn't up for the exercise and fell back onto her bed.

The problem was that she was simply feeling too much. She'd become comfortable in her cocooned life, separate from the rest of the world. Sure, she'd given up any semblance of happiness, but that also meant the overwhelming sadness she was now experiencing was kept at bay. She would take *nothing* over constant pain. It had taken years for her to put up her walls of numbness, and now they were crashing down around her.

Julian was the problem. He made her feel things she hadn't

felt in centuries. She had deadened her emotions, and Julian was forcing her to feel again. Like a moth to his flame, she was compelled to search him out, regardless of the turmoil it caused inside her.

Ellie didn't know if she even wanted to feel again. Sure, there were pleasant emotions that occurred when she was with Julian, but the rest were negative. It had been hard work burying everything, and now it looked like all her efforts were coming undone against her will.

The thought of getting her hands on the *Handbook* was the only thing keeping her moving at this point. Her desire to know how to kill vampires was all-consuming. She still hadn't decided what she was going to do with that information, but she figured she'd know once she got it.

Across the room, her phone started ringing the annoying default ring she'd never bothered to change. She didn't even need to look at the screen to know who was calling. Julian was the only person, living or dead, that called her.

"Hello?"

"Are you free?" he asked without preamble.

Not for centuries, she thought.

"Why?"

"I need you to come over."

Interest made her sit up. Maybe he had the book. "Why?" she repeated.

"It's a surprise."

She hesitated for only a moment before agreeing. "I'll be right over."

After all the times she'd gone to Julian's over the last several weeks, she had the route memorized. When she got to his house, she didn't even bother knocking, knowing it would be unlocked for her.

Pushing open the door, she was surprised by a nervous

Julian standing on the other side, waiting for her with a giant bouquet of red roses in his hands. "Surprise," he said. "I have dinner—or whatever it is at this time of day—cooking now."

Ellie stood frozen in place, stunned. Of course, there had been moments of attraction between them, but she'd never imagined he'd do something like this. She'd assumed they'd just ignore those moments. But this was a date, a real, honest date.

When she didn't immediately respond, he picked up a book with a bow on it sitting on the side table next to him. "I got you this. It covers the timeframe you're so interested in."

With numb fingers, Ellie accepted the book. It was a history of northern Spain and was about the time period she liked best. She wondered when he'd noticed such a small detail.

"I didn't really think this far ahead," he admitted. "If it isn't obvious, I've developed feelings for you during our nights together. I thought, well, I thought it was mutual, but if it isn't, I apologize and hope we can look past this."

After opening her mouth, she immediately shut it. She had no idea what she wanted to say. Did she have feelings for him? She had no idea. If her dream had been any indication, at the very least she felt desire.

Looking at it logically, she could admit he'd made her laugh and smile more than she had in decades and that was something. On the other hand, there were moments when he reminded her so much of Max that it nearly brought her to tears, and when she got home, all she could do was wallow in her guilt.

She still loved Max. That wasn't going to change. It was impossible. But when she met Julian's gaze, she had to admit there was something there—something more than just a passing fancy. Despite that, at the end of it all, there was no future for her and Julian.

But she could give him this night. He was a good person, and one night wouldn't kill her. Maybe if she was human and hadn't lost her love, they could have been happy together. It was a nice thought.

She allowed herself that little fantasy for a moment before nodding to Julian with a smile. "Let's eat."

CHAPTER SEVEN

Ellie was sure the food was delicious, and she made all the appropriate noises, but, she could barely taste it. There was nothing stopping her from eating human food, but the taste was virtually nonexistent. She had wisely mentioned to Julian before they sat down to eat that she'd had a large meal so she could pick gingerly at the minimal amount of food spread around her plate. Too much would slow her down and make her groggy.

"It sounds cliché, but I was taken with you from the moment I saw you hunched over in the bookstore," Julian said, poking at his plate. He shot her a shy smile that lit up his face.

Ellie stared at him, trying to think back to what she'd been doing. "You couldn't even see what I looked like. How long were you standing there watching me, by the way? You're lucky I don't have quicker reflexes." In truth, her reflexes were far superior to a human's, but the little white lie was warranted.

"Yeah, that wasn't ideal. But I was interested in the book you were holding too, I swear. It wasn't all about you. It just *mostly* was." Julian blushed in a charming, bashful way. "And I wasn't standing there *that* long."

Haltingly, she admitted, "I was a bit attracted to you as well."

Sensing her hesitation, he asked, "Is something wrong?"

Ellie stared at him, trying to figure out what she wanted to do. She didn't feel capable of lying to him about anything important, but she couldn't tell him the truth about her undead nature, either. He'd think she was insane, and she needed his help to find the book.

Maybe she could tell him a bit of the truth but no real details? There was nothing stopping her from telling him about Max if she left out the vampire part.

"I was in love before," she started, her gaze directed down to her plate. She couldn't do this if she had to look into Julian's understanding face. "He was my everything, and he... died. Very traumatically. And I witnessed it. I don't know if I'll ever recover from it, and right now, I'm just very confused. I don't know how I'm supposed to feel."

"I... I can't even imagine how hard that would be," Julian said.

Ellie risked a glance at him and found he was smiling at her softly. She returned the expression, and they started eating again. Her heart felt lighter now that she'd gotten that out there. It might not change anything, but Julian deserved to know the few details she could tell him. Although she might be shrouded in mystery, she didn't want to be.

"So, what about the back of me attracted you?" Ellie asked around another bite. He hadn't been able to see her face as he'd come up behind her.

"Your hair," he answered without hesitation. "How it caught the light in the shop..."

Max had loved her hair, too.

She felt a sharp pang and pushed it away. Tonight was about her and Julian. He might not know it, but they just had tonight, and she was going to make the most of it.

Julian chuckled. "Your ass wasn't half bad, either."

She looked up.

Julian laughed, the sound rich and warm, and held up both hands in a display of innocence. "Too far? I'm sorry."

She chewed the inside of her cheek, amused. "For what it's worth, I liked yours too."

He gave her a cocky smirk and leaned sideways off his chair, giving his hip a pat. "Squats."

"I meant your hair," she said.

Julian blushed for a second time, and she decided she liked making him flustered.

He cleared his throat. "My mom used to scold me for always looking a fright because I'm always running my hands through it."

"It gives you character."

"I can think of worse things to be told." His smile was so effortlessly charming, and every time he directed it at her, she felt something flutter in her chest. It was unbidden, and she couldn't control it.

Julian was bringing out these feelings, despite the emotions warring inside her. No matter how hard she tried to suppress them, they kept on sneaking their way past her defenses.

They finished dinner, bantering back and forth, before Julian took the dishes to the kitchen, refusing Ellie's offer to help. He left them in the sink, saying he'd do them when she left.

"There's something I want to show you." He grabbed her hand and pulled her upstairs, past his library's door, and into a room she hadn't visited before. She'd always either stayed downstairs or in the library. She realized it was his bedroom, but before any anxiety could take hold, he pulled her outside onto a balcony.

He smiled at her. "There are only so many stars you can see with the light pollution, but it's fairly clear tonight. You can see more than you normally can right now. I love to stand out here on nights like this. There's just something about stars that invigorate the soul."

Ellie didn't believe she had a soul any longer, but she stepped to the edge of the balcony and looked up. Compared to the number of stars she used to see in the old days before light pollution, it wasn't the prettiest sky she'd ever seen. However, its reflection in Julian's amazed eyes was undeniably beautiful, even for a cynic like her.

"I do love the stars," she mused aloud. It was incredible to think that the stars she gazed at tonight were the same stars she'd gazed at centuries years ago.

Perhaps they had died out eons ago, but their light still brightened the evening. It was comforting to know there was something as ageless as herself, perhaps more so. But it was also sad to know eventually their light would fade, whereas she would live on forever unless she had help.

"I know you love the stars," Julian said.

She turned to him, a disbelieving grin on her face. "How did you know that?"

He shrugged. "You always look up."

Once again, Ellie was astonished by what Julian noticed. When it came to her, it seemed he didn't miss anything. "I feel like you've figured out everything about me already," she teased. She had no idea what she would say if he accused her of being a vampire. Hopefully he wasn't that intuitive.

He laughed and shook his head. "I have a feeling I don't know you at all, Ellie."

"Does that bother you?"

The look he gave her set her body on fire. "No, of course not. You're a mystery I'd love to solve."

Ellie turned back to the stars and was struck by a memory of her and Max lying out beneath the stars in Asturias. She hadn't even known she still had that memory until it was upon her. Her breath caught and she felt like she'd been struck. Shaking her head, she dispelled the thought. Now wasn't the time. Now was Julian's time, not Max's.

Julian gently took Ellie's shoulder and turned her toward him. "I'd like to kiss you now, Ellie," he whispered.

Meeting his gaze, she nodded ever so slightly. Going as slow as possible to allow her the option to change her mind, Julian lowered his head until his lips just brushed hers. It was the lightest of touches, yet it was everything her dream had been and more.

A rush of emotions assailed her, and she pushed them away. She would deal with them later.

Greedily, she wrapped her hand around the back of his head and pulled him to her, capturing his lips with her own. They both groaned, their sounds mixing together into a song as old as the stars above.

With a gentle nudge of his tongue, Ellie opened her lips, deepening the kiss to something more intense. His hands gripped her waist firmly, holding her in place as if he were scared she'd run away. Desire grew within her, and she gripped him tighter. She needed to be closer to him. She needed *him*.

The thought surprised her. She realized it wasn't just that she was attracted to Julian. If sex was on the table, she wanted it.

Maybe she was old-fashioned, but she didn't take sex lightly. It was something from the old days that had stuck with her over the years. There had been a few men since Max that she'd used to try to make herself feel better, but those one-offs had only ever made her feel worse, and before long, she gave up.

Max's face flashed behind her closed eyes, and Ellie gasped, pulling away from Julian on instinct, just like in her dream.

She loved Max, and despite what she may feel for this intriguing new man, there could be no real future for them. He was human. He would grow old and die, leaving her all alone again. She had promised herself long ago she would never make another vampire and that was a promise she had every intention of keeping. The guilt would eat her alive.

She opened her eyes, and to her relief, Julian was still himself. She stared up at him, and he seemed more puzzled than offended. Ellie realized her heart had been shattered long ago and there was no putting it back together. There was something broken inside her that couldn't be fixed by anyone.

"I can't do this," she whispered before she turned and fled. The memory of Julian's confused, hurt face followed her as she made her way out of his house.

It was close to three in the morning, and Ellie knew from experience that most of the people still out at that time were up to no good, which made them easy pickings for her.

If anything was going to distract her it would be feeding. Usually, she pushed her body to its limits when it came to the time in between feedings. If she didn't eat often enough, her baser instincts would take over and that was a dangerous situation for everyone. She had to monitor her body and be very careful, but normally she walked the line well.

It had been a long time since she'd been disgusted by blood. When she'd first been turned, feeding had been a struggle for her. She'd been scared of blood and the thought of drinking straight from the source made her ill. She'd taken blood from a cup for years. It was easier to pretend it was grape juice that way.

Now she didn't even think when she sank her fangs into someone. Part of that was knowing she only targeted criminals and people who deserved some retribution. The memories that flashed into her mind when she drank were usually dark, but she'd learned to deal with that as well. It was amazing what someone could get used to over time and exposure.

She was several blocks from Julian's house when she felt the presence of someone behind her. They may have been unobserved by a human target, but Ellie was a different story. With her enhanced abilities, he might as well have had a neon sign announcing his arrival.

She slowed down on purpose, allowing him to catch up to her. Seconds before he grabbed her to pull them into the alley they were passing, she turned. He was so surprised by her sudden movement that he didn't even resist when she pulled him into the dark.

The force tore his shoulder from its socket. His eyes widened in shock and his lips parted, daring to let loose a scream, but Ellie silenced him by flashing her fangs in the moonlight. The sound that escaped his lips was nothing more than a pitiful whimper as he tried to pull away. She tightened her grip, hushed him the way a mother might a sleeping babe, and drew him in like they were slow dancing.

His whimpers quickened as he fought back panic. Hunger rippled through her. *Yes. Blood.* She could smell him, rich and sweet, and feel the heat radiating from his body. Julian's dinner had left her unsatiated, but this lurking predator would fill her to the brim with contentment.

She opened her mouth wide, letting her fangs extend further.

"N-no," the man gasped. "Please!"

She bore down. Her fangs pierced his neck. He let out a strangled cry before giving way to gurgling sounds as she drew great gulps of his life's blood down her throat. He thrashed momentarily before going limp in her arms, and she lowered him to the ground, where he paled with every passing second. His eyes glazed over as he stared up at the starry night sky she and Julian had admired together not a half hour earlier.

She drained the last drop, ran her finger along her bottom

lip to clean up, and rose to her feet, leaving the corpse in the middle of the alley with his dislocated arm splayed awkwardly to one side. Ellie licked the remnants of blood from her finger and felt her senses stretch like lazy cats in the morning sun.

She wanted more, and where one creep hunted, there was bound to be another.

CHAPTER EIGHT

It came as no surprise to Ellie that Julian tried to contact her almost immediately. She'd turned her phone off while she was hunting. By the time she got home and turned her phone back on, she had three missed calls from him.

Without hesitation, she cleared the notifications without listening to any of the voicemails. She didn't care what he had to say. His messages would only cause her pain she didn't want to feel. He'd made her feel again, and she cursed him for it. Life would be so much easier if she was still numb.

There was no happily ever after for them, so there was no reason to pretend otherwise, even for a short period of time. She could find a copy of the book on her own. She didn't need his help.

She'd gone through enough of Julian's collection to know it held no real value to her. It had been a nice diversion while it lasted, but now, she was firmly back in the real world.

To distract herself, she picked her phone back up and started looking for a copy of the handbook. After several hours, she chucked her phone across the room, agitated. She couldn't find anything anywhere. No trace of a posting existed.

To her horror, Julian called her daily.

How annoying.

It was hard getting over someone when they insisted on trying to get in touch with her. She was just grateful she had never invited him over. She had the sinking suspicion that if she had, he would show up on her doorstep.

She made the mistake of listening to one of his messages, and it had hurt worse than she'd expected. It was clear he cared for her and was hurting, and those two things were almost too much for her to bear. Outside of Julian, when had there been a time someone had actually cared about her? The answer was obvious. Since Max had been murdered, there'd been no one. She'd been all alone for hundreds of years.

As the weeks went by, he called less and less. She never answered, and after a while, he seemed to take the hint. Despite what Ellie told herself, she felt some grief, but she accepted it as something she deserved. She'd hurt him both with her actions and her inactions, and she didn't see any way they could come back from that. She didn't belong in his life, and the sooner he realized that, the better off they'd be.

It had been over a week since he'd last called when she heard her phone ding. She rolled over on her bed and stared at her phone on the pillow next to her. She was about to delete it unread when her eyes scanned over the previews without her permission. If he was sending her a farewell message, she didn't really want to read it.

I found it.

Shooting up out of bed, she stared at her phone. She clicked on the message, but there was nothing more to it, just those three simple words.

He had to be talking about *The Vampire Hunter's Handbook*. How had he found it? She'd still been actively searching for it and hadn't found any listings for it anywhere. Her mind was racing, hopping from question to question before any answers could be determined.

Unlike the last time she had been here, she knocked on the door when she got to Julian's place. It swung open moments later to reveal the man himself. Backlit, he looked like he was glowing, and her heart twisted in knots. No matter what she'd tried to convince herself of, she'd missed him.

"Hi."

"Hi," he murmured back, eating her up with his gaze.

Ellie cleared her throat, and Julian stepped aside to allow her entrance. She slipped inside and paused.

"I didn't think you'd come, to be honest," Julian said, not meeting her gaze. "You didn't answer any of my messages, so I thought you might have blocked my number."

She stared at him. "I didn't block you," she finally said. "I didn't even consider it."

"Well, that's something, I guess," he muttered. If she'd been a human, she'd have missed his comment but with her superior hearing, she still caught it. He folded his arms over his chest. "Is the book really that important to you?"

She nodded. "I've been searching for it for forever."

He sighed, as if that answered whatever question he had. "Can we talk about what happened the other night?"

"It wasn't the other night, it was weeks ago," Ellie said, pointing out the obvious.

His glare burned into her. "You know what I mean, Ellie. Can we talk about what happened?"

She opened her mouth and then shut it. This was not a conversation she actually wanted to have with him, but she didn't know how to avoid it. He had the greatest gift anyone could give her—the handbook. From this point forward, her life would change until it was unrecognizable. She had used hundreds of people over the years before Julian. She could use him, too.

She decided to give him half of the truth. "I realized we have no future together, and I don't want to waste your time when you can find someone who actually can be with you."

He ran his hand through his hair, messing it up more than it already was. It stuck out every which way. No wonder his mother used to scold him. "But I don't want anyone else, Ellie. I want you. And why are you convinced we have no future together? That's just not true."

Shaking her head, Ellie frowned. "You don't know me, Julian, not really. It just wouldn't work out between us."

"Then let me learn about you! Let me know you, Ellie! You don't have to be so afraid of getting hurt again. I'm not going anywhere."

She wore her calmness like a cloak. "You don't know what you're talking about, and I can't explain it to you, as much as I would like to. Just trust me on this, Julian." She tried to soften herself for his sake. "Please."

He pinched the bridge of his nose, and after a long moment, he nodded. "Let's just get this over with."

Ellie relaxed a bit and took a step past him before freezing. She wasn't sure where to go, and she didn't want to assume it was in his library. It could have been in the office she'd glanced into once.

"It's in the library," Julian said, judging her hesitation correctly. Besides Max, who had read her like an open book, Julian was the only other person that could read her so well. It was both a blessing and a curse.

Ellie nodded and started up the stairs, Julian close behind her. She had so much she wanted to tell him, but everything she had to say would make things more complicated. Her biggest regret was that she couldn't tell him what she truly was.

So many questions would be answered if she just told him

she was a vampire, but she doubted he'd believe her, even with a demonstration. Worse, that might not be enough to scare him off. After spending so much time with him, Ellie had the feeling he'd find a real live vampire more interesting than fear-inspiring, which was the opposite of what she wanted.

After entering his library, Ellie's gaze immediately flicked to the large tome sitting on his desk. It was thicker than she'd expected. She eyed the leather cover. It was rumored the books were bound in vampire skin. From this distance, she wasn't certain of anything, but from the looks of it, it seemed the rumors were true.

Gross.

With a reverence that bordered on uncertainty, she inched closer until she was standing before it. She saw he hadn't managed to find an English translation. This one was in Cyrillic.

"I can't read it, but the seller swore it was the right book," Julian said, walking over to the desk and staring down at it. He looked a bit green, and Ellie wondered if he'd heard the rumors about the binding as well. At the very least he didn't seem inclined to touch it.

Probably wise, she thought.

"It is," Ellie whispered, lightly tracing the title. The leather felt weird beneath her fingers, foreign and familiar all at once. She wondered which poor soul made up the cover of this book. Perhaps more than one vampire's flesh comprised the binding and cover.

"Can you read Cyrillic?" Julian asked, surprise tinging his words. He was gazing at her intently, as if he'd just gotten the surprise of a lifetime.

"I speak several languages besides English. Spanish is actually my first language." With ever-cold fingers, she opened the book and scanned the first page. It was in excellent condition, and she wondered again where Julian had found it when she had found nothing up until this point. How could he have better results than her?

Julian looked impressed. "Wow. You don't even have an accent. That's incredible."

Although the desire to get the book had been her own, there was excitement lacing his words. Somewhere along the way, he'd become invested in finding it, and he seemed genuinely excited that they now had it before them.

"Julian… I've looked for this for so long. You have no idea what this means to me." She bit her bottom lip and spared a glance up at him. The dim light of the library cast shadows across his face, making his features look sharper. "Thank you for this, especially after everything…"

After how I hurt you, she thought regretfully.

He slid his hands into his pockets. "I knew your hunt for the book was more important than what happened between us. I spared only a moment's thought on not telling you before I sent the message. I needed you to see it, too."

She put her hand on his and squeezed gratefully. He slipped his fingers between hers. His lips looked so soft, and the hardness of his anger had softened since coming up to the library. Had he forgiven her so quickly? He nodded down at the book, encouraging her to continue investigating it, but she only had eyes for him and those perfect lips of his.

Before she realized what she was doing, she stretched to the tips of her toes and kissed him. The relief and pleasure were fleeting. Guilt flooded her.

You're playing with him, Eleonor.

She pulled away, disgusted with herself.

Now, more than ever, there was no future for them. With the book in her possession, it was only a matter of time before she wasn't around anymore. Either she'd use the knowledge contained in the book to kill herself or she'd go back to Europe and make her betrayers pay. Neither option had room for Julian. How dare she let him think otherwise yet again.

With shaking hands, she picked up the book. "I promise I'll pay you twice what it's worth. Just name your price." Taking the books into her arms, she turned away from him, toward the door.

"Is this it?" he asked. He didn't sound sad. He sounded resigned, which was somehow worse. Against her better judgment, she turned and met Julian's gaze. In it, she saw the future they could have had, if she was someone else. Anyone else. She would be happy, and they'd have several decades together before he died. After, she could go back to her revenge plan, either killing herself or her enemies. It wasn't like her prey was going to die on her.

A memory flashed before her eyes of her and Max on the night they'd professed their love for one another. They'd promised each other eternity, and that was what she'd give him whether he was here or not. There wasn't room for Julian.

She cared for Julian, but Max had been her life. Turning without answering, she left, her grip tight on the book that would be her savior. She'd leave him the money in his mailbox in the middle of the night and slip away. It was what she did best, after all.

CHAPTER NINE

Ellie walked with the book in a vise grip against her chest. She finally had it, the end to all her suffering. No more aimless suicide attempts that didn't end in the black nothingness she longed for. No more leaping off bridges, throwing herself onto fires, biting into her own wrists, or silver bullets to the brain.

Peace had never been so close.

But the joy she expected to feel, or at least the closest thing to joy she ever expected to feel since Max was alive, never came. As she walked, the image of Julian's resigned and pained face flashed before her eyes. She had to admit, at least to herself, that she cared deeply for him. She'd been miserable over the weeks they'd been separated and walking away from him was one of the hardest things she'd ever done. Just because it was the right thing to do didn't make it easy.

She balked at using the word *love*, because that wasn't what this was, but she knew she felt something close to it for him. She felt like she'd known him for centuries already—like they'd both made homes in each other's souls and truly learned each other, the way she had with Max.

Max. She'd promised to always love him, and as long as she was alive—or whatever she was—so was that promise. The thought of betraying Max made her insides riot. A human could never grasp the bond between a pair of vampires who were in love. It was beyond their comprehension. But Ellie had felt that love and lived those days with Max. They didn't just disappear because she felt a semblance of that love for Julian three hundred years later.

Her final moments with Max surfaced in her memories, and she flinched, remembering the sting of the arrow in her chest and the wild desperation she'd felt. She'd been prepared to fight if needed, whatever it took to get them both out of there. The odds meant nothing to her. Despite everything, Max had been calm. He'd told her to run, knowing he wouldn't make it out with her. Looking back, it seemed he'd known he was going to die that night, and his calm demeanor was a testament to his character and who he was as a person.

Above all, Max wanted her to live, whether he was by her side or not. But would he have wanted her to live as she had been living over the years? Shunning the world so she wouldn't get hurt again, but also locking herself away from all joy?

Ashamed, she knew the answer was no. He would have wanted her to be happy in whatever form it took. He'd always wanted what was best for her and that didn't stop just because he was no longer here. She knew with certainty that if he was here today, he would still want what was best for her.

Ellie froze, sudden realization striking her like an arrow. It wasn't loyalty to Max that kept her from Julian. It was the fear of losing him, even if it was just to old age.

It was her own fear stopping her from experiencing something wonderful. She knew Julian would make their time together memorable and he'd do everything in his power to make her happy. He was a good man, and those were hard to come by. The odds that she would come across two were slim.

Did she want her remaining time to be miserable or should she take the chance on happiness with Julian?

Making her decision, she turned on her heel and all but ran back to Julian's. After pounding on the door, she feared he wouldn't answer, or worse, he would think she was someone nefarious and call the cops. After what felt like several lifetimes, the lock clicked and Julian opened the door. He must have seen her through the peephole.

"What—" He was cut off by Ellie flinging herself at him and kissing him with everything she had, trying to convey all the things she wasn't strong enough to put into words. He let out a small squeak, the force of her embrace expelling air from his lungs. She mumbled an apology against his lips and loosened her hold.

Once Julian could breathe again, he returned her enthusiasm, wrapping his arms around her. The book was stuck between them, keeping them from pressing against one another fully.

Pulling back, she closed the door and set the book on the side table where it would be safe. The book had only just left her fingers when Julian was kissing her again, this time matching her intensity. She opened her mouth, and he swept in, exploring her thoroughly. A sense of rightness flooded through her, and Ellie knew she'd made the right decision, no matter how hard it had been.

Pulling back, he kissed down the side of her neck, nipping the sensitive flesh gently. She shivered in pleasure and had to fight back the urge to extend her fangs. The scent of his blood teased her, a silent dare to take more than he was offering, but after her recent feed, she pushed the rush of bloodlust down.

Her eager fingers started tugging on the edge of Julian's t-shirt, and they broke apart long enough for her to pull the offending garment over his head and toss it across the room.

Despite herself, Ellie was impressed. She'd always known

that Julian had a nice body, but now the proof was before her. With light fingers, she stroked down his chest, admiring the way the muscles rippled at her touch. He stood still and allowed her to explore his body.

With a growl, Julian fell back onto the couch, taking Ellie with him so she straddled his lap. Evidence of his arousal pressed against her warmth, and she squirmed, the friction causing both of them to groan.

"You're wearing too much," Julian growled, pulling at her top.

Anxious to feel skin on skin, she helped him remove her shirt and the sports bra she'd thrown on. She wished she'd had the foresight to put on something better, something with lace. Weren't all human men attracted to lace?

Human men care more about what's under the lace, she thought.

Julian was transfixed, his hands gently cupping her breasts. With reverence, he leaned forward and took one nipple into his mouth, swirling it with his tongue before giving it a gentle bite. Ellie gasped, the sensations foreign and almost too much. It had been years—decades—since she'd been touched in such a manner. She didn't know what to do, so she buried her hands in Julian's hair. As he turned his attention to her other breast, she threw her head back. The sensation was exquisite and electric, and a thousand times more intense than what her human female counterpart might experience.

Poor humans.

"Julian," she moaned, the sound throaty.

"Yes?" he murmured against her flesh, the sound caressing her wet nipple.

"I think we're both wearing too much clothing."

She felt his laugh as much as she heard it. "First one naked is in charge," Julian said, sliding her off him and standing in record time.

Stunned, it took her a couple of seconds to process what he

said. Then she was up and tossing away her pants. By the time she was naked, Julian was standing there before her, the overhead lighting glinting upon his golden hair. His erection stood out against his body, and Ellie's mouth watered. She wanted to taste it and could already imagine how the hard flesh would move in her mouth—and deep inside her.

She stepped forward, reaching for his cock, and Julian stepped out of her reach. "Nope. I won. Get on the couch."

Apparently, the man was no longer timid with his affection for her. It was like a dam had burst and he couldn't hide how much he wanted her. For half a second, she thought of disobeying, but she really wanted to know what he had in mind, so she did as she was told. Besides, he deserved to feel a little power, didn't he? And he didn't have to know that she could have overpowered him in seconds and had him whichever way she pleased. It would only hurt his feelings.

Julian crawled in between her legs, spreading them further. His knees pressed against her inner thighs. Did he notice how cold her flesh was?

"Beautiful." With slow movements, he lowered his head and kissed up one thigh and then the other.

"Julian," she whined, panting. Such a simple thing turned her on so much.

"What do you want?" he whispered mere inches from her glistening center. She could feel the exhale of the words.

"Please," she begged, her voice breaking.

Julian pulled back so he could meet her fevered gaze. "What do you want?"

"I need your mouth on me," she commanded. Julian grazed his lips against her slit and began to suckle at her core. All thoughts flew from Ellie's mind, her entire existence boiling down to what the man between her legs was doing.

She moaned as Julian slipped one finger into her and found her clit simultaneously. Bliss washed over her, and after a few more moments, Ellie spiraled into ecstasy, her orgasm crashing through her.

Once she'd stopped quaking, Julian raised his head and smiled at her, pleased with his work.

"My turn," Ellie said, scooting off the couch and dropping to her knees before him. He turned, and she gently gripped his cock at its base. Starting at the base, she licked her way up, making sure her teeth stayed tucked away. The last thing she wanted was to accidentally bite Julian's erection. The trouble was, the more pleasure she felt, the more her bloodlust spiraled together with her sexual desire. If she wasn't careful, the two could become one, and she could lose herself to the moment.

She'd never lost control before, but then again, no mortal man had ever made her feel like this, either.

When she got to the tip, she opened her mouth wide and sank her mouth down, gagging a little when the tip of his cock hit the back of her throat and slid down a bit. She now understood where his charisma came from, and she had to squeeze her thighs together at the thought of him entering her.

With steady up-and-down motions, she worked his cock, going deeper and deeper until Julian suddenly pulled her back. "I'm going to cum if you don't stop," he hissed, his eyes wild with desire.

Pleased, Ellie smiled and stood. She motioned him back and lowered herself down onto his lap.

"Wait. I don't have a condom," Julian said, trying to push her off him.

"I'm on the pill," Ellie lied. She wasn't, but she was also dead. She knew for a fact she didn't have a heartbeat, and in order to get pregnant, you needed a living mother. There was no risk of accidents here.

When he nodded, she positioned him at her entrance and slowly lowered herself down an inch or two. Her body fought back against the intrusion for a moment before giving way, allowing her to slide down the length of him to his base.

They froze, staring into each other's eyes. There was no coming back from this, and they both knew it.

Any and all thoughts fled from Ellie's mind when Julian grabbed her hips and started moving. Each stroke heightened the fire burning inside her. She'd already cum once, but she felt the spiral starting almost immediately. Faster than she thought possible, she was being thrown off the edge. In her ecstasy, she leaned down and nibbled gently at Julian's earlobe. He let out a low, primal growl that spurred her on. Her lips trailed down to his neck, grazing his fluttering pulse as he thrust deep inside her. Her teeth sang against his flesh. Delirious pleasure built up inside her, so intense and hot that it distracted her from the way her fangs extended and his skin gave way, breaking under her bite.

Bite.

Blood rushed into her mouth, and the memories came fast and pure. She was in the bed she had shared with Max, staring down at herself in the middle of sex, her fangs completely out. Glancing to the right, she realized she *was* Max.

She was Max, watching the most intimate moment happening between them.

What the hell is going on?

CHAPTER TEN

Coming down from the high that Julian had taken her to was painful. They lay in a panting heap on the couch, both trying to catch their breath. Neither had the will to move quite yet as they calmed down.

If Ellie was lucky, Julian would think she'd just bit him and leave it at that. The two puncture wounds she'd caused were tiny, and unless he craned his neck at an unnatural angle, he wouldn't be able to see them. She only hoped no one at the school would point them out to him. That might be enough for him to put two and two together.

His blood had tasted so good.

Too good.

It still lingered on her tongue like an endless dessert.

"Wow," Julian groaned as Ellie started rising off him.

"Hmm," she hummed, trying to keep her unease at bay. The last thing she needed to do was freak Julian out and then not be able to explain what was wrong. She'd already jerked him around too much. "I need to use the restroom to clean up." On her way out of the room, she grabbed her clothing and tossed Julian's boxers to him. They hit him square in the face and he peeled them away. She stole a glance over her shoulder and saw him smiling contently with his eyes closed.

In the bathroom, she cleaned herself up and then splashed cold water on her face in an effort to clear her head a bit. She was reeling and knew she wouldn't be able to answer any questions Julian might have about what this all meant.

She had no clue what it meant either. Before she'd seen a memory from Max's point of view, she'd been taking charge of her own happiness. Now? She was confused and lost. What should have been just between her and Julian was now between the three of them, and the worst part was Julian couldn't know that. There was no way to explain to him how a dead man had come between what had just happened without sounding like a crazy person.

Taking one last look at her reflection, Ellie exited the restroom. She found Julian in the kitchen staring into his fridge. "Do you want a snack?" He patted his stomach. "I really worked up an appetite. You must be famished, too. It's important to nourish yourself after all that." He pumped his eyebrows playfully.

Max had always pushed her to feed when he noticed signs of hunger. The way Julian wanted to take care of her reminded her of her Max.

Ellie shook her head. "I actually need to go. I have some stuff I need to take care of tonight. It can't exactly wait. I just came back because, well, you know. I figured some stuff out, I guess, but if you ask me about it now, I won't be able to tell you."

Have some damn conviction, Ellie, she thought sourly.

Julian turned to her, a frown on his face. He inspected her, and she made sure to keep her face blank. "Okay," he said. Without hesitation, he leaned down and kissed her. "I'll talk to you soon, okay? Go do whatever you have to do, but don't forget about me this time, please."

She nodded and forced a smile before turning and heading out, making sure to grab the book on her way past the end table.

Once out in the night air, she felt a bit better. At least she felt as if she could think better being outside of the place that smelled like Julian and sex. Picking a random direction, she started walking, deep in thought. There were still hours of night left, and she didn't have any place to be.

Every time vampires bit someone, they saw a flash of their memories. The victim's memories. As far as anyone knew, those memories were random and could be at any point in the victim's life. It wasn't necessarily the last thing they'd thought about. There was no correlation, and this was one field where extensive research had been done.

When Ellie bit her victims, she didn't get to choose to see a nice memory. In fact, she usually saw horrible things the person had done, but that was because she picked horrible people to feed from.

So why had she seen something from Max's point of view when she'd bit Julian?

For half a second, she convinced herself that it was her own memory she'd seen, but then she remembered the angle and how she'd stared down at her own body, like she had been seeing through Max's eyes. She remembered that moment with Max perfectly. They'd had a fight and had thoroughly enjoyed making up.

It definitely wasn't one of Julian's memories. He wouldn't be born for several hundred years after that evening, long after Max had died. Besides, the reflection in the mirror had been of Max, not of Julian. Julian didn't even know what Max looked like. When he'd borrowed the book by Javier Rodriquez, he hadn't noticed the portrait that looked just like her. That portrait would be the only image of Max that Julian had been exposed to.

What was she missing? Something was going on, and she felt

like whatever it was, it was hiding just out of sight. Usually, she was great at figuring things out on her own, but this time, she was struggling.

For once, she wished she still had a Coven to help her. Not hers. They'd betrayed her. But other vampires she could bounce ideas off of. In the grand scheme of things, she was a relatively young vampire. Some were thousands of years old, who knew more about the world than anyone else in existence.

Getting a straight answer out of one of the Elders was easier said than done, though. They didn't think the same way those younger than them did anymore. If she had to guess, they didn't think or see time as linear, and that made communication very hard. It was like talking to a living riddle.

If she had friends or family, she could talk to them. But she was alone. She wouldn't even know where to turn to for advice if she had the capacity to form a coherent thought. The only friend she had was Julian, and he didn't even know vampires were real, let alone their inner workings.

Perhaps I could have spent some of these hundred years looking for others like me instead of throwing myself off of bridges, she mused, gripping the tome tighter to her chest.

Searching her brain, she tried to think of any instance where memories of someone else was in another's body and she came up with nothing. Even the whispered things she'd overheard growing up hadn't dealt with this kind of thing. Growing up in a Coven as the leader's daughter, much was hidden from her, but over time, she'd learned the best ways to listen in on conversations and had heard plenty she shouldn't have.

There was something she was missing, but she had no clue what it was. When she finally got home, she placed the *Handbook* on her bed and turned to the books she had piled in the corner of what a human might have used as a living room. It had an electric fireplace she'd never switched on or bothered to clean. The faux stones, jagged and on-trend from ten years ago, were muted from a layer of dust. She made a mental note to acquire a bookcase. Some of the books in her collection were very valuable and probably deserved a place off the floor.

All her books involved vampires of one kind or another, so she would have to sort them some other way in order to be useful. Maybe those that involved information on feeding versus those that didn't?

After several minutes of sorting, she realized that almost all the books included at least one section on feeding because it was a basic function of vampires. Throwing her hands up in frustration, Ellie stood and stretched before sitting back down, determined to figure things out.

With renewed vigor, she stared at the books strewn all around her. How had someone else's memory gotten placed inside Julian's body? Because that was what must have happened. It had to be. Although it didn't make sense, it made more sense than the other options.

Her eyes widened. What if it was just a different body but the same person? What if Max had been reincarnated? Was that even possible?

You're grasping at straws, Ellie.

Trying not to get too excited, she searched through her stacks of books for one in particular. After checking all the books in the room, she felt like throwing something. Besides the book from Javier Rodriquez that held her portrait, she owned a second book by him, one on his musings about philosophy and religion. But where had she put it?

Shooting up, she practically ran to her closet. It was tiny, but she had a half memory of placing the few books she had on religion in the back to get them away from her. Throwing several pairs of shoes out of the way, Ellie found the stack of books and pulled them out. The one she was looking for was right on top.

Relieved she hadn't lost the book, she grabbed it and flopped onto her bed. She skimmed the first couple of pages and found they were full of religious concepts.

There were two types of vampires, those that weren't religious and those that were. It seemed weird to consider that a damned creature of the night might still believe in God, but there were those that did. She guessed it was easier to believe there was an all-powerful being looking out for everyone when you were a supernatural being yourself. Besides, most of them hadn't chosen to be this way, and those that resented their new life as a vampire still clung to the version of themselves when they used to be as humans. Religion, the church, and all those old familiarities could be a comfort.

Before she had turned, she'd been very pious, but after her transformation, she'd turned away from religion. Max was the one who believed there was some cosmic force looking out for them. To Ellie, it made more sense that if there was a God, he was an absent one. A loving God wouldn't make their creations suffer the way humanity did.

Knowing that Javier Rodriquez was a vampire gave credibility to his musings. He made it clear in the first couple of pages that the book contained nothing more than his observations and thoughts, and Ellie appreciated the warning. Despite this, she knew Javier knew more than he was saying. After all, a supernatural being was probably the best investigator for a supernatural occurrence. Like goes to like, after all.

Was that why she was attracted to Julian? Because there was something supernatural about him? She considered this possibility briefly before deciding she'd be attracted to him no matter what. He was a very handsome man.

Thinking of Julian, she checked her phone and saw she had a text message from him. Realizing he was just saying hello, she shot back a short message saying she was going to sleep. She'd lost all track of time cooped up in her dingy basement. The sun had probably risen hours ago. It was a miracle he'd accepted her strange sleeping habits so readily. Normal people would be a bit concerned.

Turning back to the book, she flipped through it, scanning each page carefully for key words. Finally, she found it —reincarnation.

CHAPTER ELEVEN

Sitting on her floor and leaning up against her mattress, Ellie considered the book in her hands. Maybe she had a sixth sense after all these years, but she figured that whatever she found in this book would probably change her world, and by extension Julian's.

Assuming it would be best to start at the beginning, Ellie flipped to the first page and started reading.

Over the years, I've come across a wide array of beliefs on what happens after death. Every religion or even those who don't subscribe to a belief system have a belief about what happens after death. It's one of the great mysteries of the universe and only those that have died know what happens. Unfortunately, that also means we have no way to contact them and ask, if they'd even answer us. Psychics and witches that communicate with the dead have yet to be proven real, despite knowing that vampires exist and that we aren't the only creatures that prowl the night.

Most people believe there is something more beyond death, that dying isn't the end of everything. A common belief across several regions is that when the body dies the soul lives on and moves on to whatever's next. The central idea here is that the soul is separate from the body and is its own consciousness. The two coexist when the person is alive but are separate after death.

What happens to the soul is a different question and depends on the religion to which you subscribe. Christendom believes in heaven and a future judgment day. Jesus and his death and resurrection are key components of their faith. Not only is there a heaven, but there's also a hell that you can be sent to if you are morally bankrupt.

There are many religions that believe in an afterlife and the majority of these believe in some sort of judgment. Take the ancient Egyptians as an example. They believed your heart records all the good and bad things you do throughout your life, and it has to be lighter than a feather in order to move on to a favorable place.

All religions have one (or many) gods or deities who have some impact on their lives. What someone believes changes the level of involvement of their god(s) in their daily lives. Some believe their god(s) to be involved in everything, and others may believe in higher powers but think they are more observers than participants in their daily life.

As a supernatural being myself, I feel almost qualified to consider the existence of God or gods. One supernatural being to another. The difficult thing with proving any god's existence is determining what is an act of god and what is an act of nature. Everything can be boiled down to an act of nature. Just because something is statistically unlikely doesn't make it impossible. We live on a flying ball of rock circling a ball of fire in a giant abyss of nothing. Depending on your belief system, this could be proof either for or against a deity. So where do acts of god fall? That is the question.

Ellie skipped over the next section, skimming for key words. It wasn't that she wasn't interested in what Rodriquez had to say. It was that she was searching for something specific. Maybe at a later date, she'd come back and peruse his writings about theism, but right then, she was on a mission. Flipping quickly through the book, she then slowed down around halfway when the section was labeled "On Death and Beyond." When she spotted *reincarnation*, she went back to the beginning of that paragraph.

Out of all possible outcomes after death, the only option that holds any real value to me is reincarnation. For Christian nations, this might seem outlandish, but at the end of the day, it is the most logical conclusion. Let me explain myself.

There are multiple religions that consider reincarnation a key element of their faith. Buddhism, Hinduism, Jainism, and Sikhism all subscribe to the belief of reincarnation after death. By definition, reincarnation is the rebirth of a soul into a new body.

There's a certain sense to it. If the soul cannot be destroyed except through violent events like transformations into a vampire, it only makes sense that they come back to us in some way. Souls are hardy things in most cases, and all religions recognize this fact.

As vampires, we are privy to the memories of our victims when we feed from them. Which memories will be revealed is still unknown, despite several well-known researchers working on it. The general consensus is that they are chosen at random or have some sort of meaning to the victim. If it wasn't clear, we have no idea. That being said, I've come across several memories that didn't belong to the body they were in.

The first was several hundred years ago and still sits heavy on my heart. While feeding from an elderly Chinese woman, I found she held memories of living on the streets in ancient Egypt. To say I was surprised would be an understatement. As far as I could tell, the woman had never left her little town, and the Egyptian people were far more advanced than what I saw in her memories. There was no reason those memories should be present, and it was my first introduction to the possibility that reincarnation was an option for a soul. It took many months of consideration to come to this conclusion, but after careful thought, I decided to be alert for other memories that didn't belong to the person I was feeding from.

I must admit that prior to this occasion, I often tried to block out the images that came unbidden. I'm already drinking someone's life force. The least I can do is allow them what little privacy I can. After this experience, I vowed to watch out for other anomalies and stopped trying to resist the pulls of the memory. In fact, I paid special attention to them, considering every angle of every memory.

It was at least a hundred years later that I was feeding on an English general when I was suddenly viewing a memory as an Italian woman. At first, I was confused and thought he might have visited Italy at some point, which would have been a normal endeavor, but then I realized the general in the memory was in fact a woman. In my careful consideration of reincarnation, it had never occurred to me that the sex of the body you are resurrected in may change.

It got me thinking about what the individuals themselves remember or if they are just as surprised by the memory as I am. Are they aware of these memories hidden deep inside themselves, or is it a total shock for them to experience said memories as I do? How traumatizing would it be to not only be a vampire's snack but also realize you have memories that don't belong to you?

The memories in both cases did not last long, just long enough to establish where and who they were before the memory slipped away. Do all humans have this remembered past? I do not know. What I do know is that every decade or so I come across another person with another memory that doesn't belong. It's happened often enough that I would say that they are not entirely uncommon. Before this, I believe that I'd never paid close enough attention to the memories shown to me and I wonder what I've missed by doing so.

What does this mean for vampires? That, I cannot say. Our souls are destroyed in the process of becoming a vampire and therefore cannot be added to a new body. With the key component missing, it just wouldn't work. Our souls carry the essence of who we are, and without it, we are nothing.

It seems we lose far more in our transformation than previously thought. If resurrection is the main aspect of the afterlife, then when we die, there is truly nothing for us. So much is given up, often without our consent. Very few ask to become vampires. Most are given no choice and must live with the consequences of something that was forced upon them.

Ellie stopped reading and laid the book on her lap. Thinking over what she'd just read, she realized that Max, as a vampire, wouldn't have the option to reincarnate, at least according to Rodriquez. His soul would have gone back to nothingness, or at least whatever happened to vampires when they died. The key to reincarnation was an intact soul, and neither she nor Max had that.

But that didn't explain the memory she'd seen when she'd bitten Julian. She had been Max, and she'd seen herself through his eyes. There was no way Julian could have gotten hold of that memory unless his soul had once been Max's. If that was the case, then the entire understanding of vampires' lack of souls had to go out the window. It would imply that they did have souls and they didn't die with the body. It seemed unlikely. How had so many vampire scientists missed this over the years?

The vampire soul, or what was left of it, was destroyed with the body. That was one of the reasons why killing another vampire was so difficult. Besides not being able to directly kill a vampire as one, indirectly killing one ensured they were gone forever, which some might say was a fate worse than death. It wasn't like vampires were lining up to be killed so someone with an Ouija board could try to contact them.

Did this mean that the entire understanding was wrong, or was Max just different? Not only had he been incredibly gifted, but he'd also been a genuinely good vampire. He might have been overconfident and cocky at times, but he'd been nothing but kind and generous, two things she'd always admired about him. If anyone deserved a second chance, it was Max. For the first time, she allowed hope to flit into her chest and take hold.

If Max was special, did this give her a second chance with him, or was this just fate or God taunting her? Was she destined to fall for a human man that didn't remember the past they'd shared? Was Julian even Max, or were they two separate entities entirely?

Reincarnation wasn't cut and dry, and she felt annoyed at the lack of available answers. She wanted definite facts that would make sense and apply to her situation.

Setting the book aside, Ellie put her head in her hands. Her mind raced with all the possibilities and implications, and she felt overwhelmed. Rodriquez had given her hope, but at the same time, there was a desperate edge to it. She knew that some of what she was feeling was the hope she would get her lover back, but that wasn't likely. At no point had Rodriquez talked about the human remembering their past lives. He'd simply stated that the memories were present. He didn't even know if the person was aware these memories existed.

Did she want Julian to remember Max's memories? She didn't know. She'd done things she wasn't proud of since he'd been gone, and she didn't want Max to find out about them. He wouldn't judge her for them, but she didn't want him to be disappointed in her. Maybe it was for the best that it was unlikely Julian would remember.

On the other hand, if he did remember, what happened to Julian? He'd lived a full life and had his own personality, no matter how similar it sometimes mirrored Max's. He had a family he loved.

Scooting onto the bed, Ellie closed her eyes and tried to calm her racing thoughts.

CHAPTER TWELVE

After reading the book, Ellie had fallen into an uneasy sleep filled with wild dreams that combined both Julian and Max into grotesque statues. Normally she didn't dream at all, and this change from the normal felt like a punishment.

Ellie felt guilty when she finally found her phone the next morning. In her hurry to research the night before, she'd flung it and it had landed between her mattress and the wall. It took her several minutes to finally locate it. She wasn't surprised at all to find Julian had been trying to get ahold of her nonstop and she had numerous missed calls and text messages.

After shooting him a quick text letting him know she was okay and asking if she could come over, she got in the shower, letting the cold spray ease her jumbled thoughts.

She spent the time in the shower contemplating whether or not she should try to help Max—Julian—get his memories back. The only thing stopping her was the consideration that perhaps remembering his old life might have some negative repercussions that she hadn't considered yet. Could a human mind handle that kind of knowledge without breaking? She didn't know. She wasn't even human anymore and it was a tough concept to wrap her head around. What would it do to Julian? The last thing she wanted to do was break his mind. That was counterintuitive.

On the other hand, if he really was Max, didn't he deserve to know who he'd once been? It wasn't like his past self had been a murderer or something. Max had been a good vampire and, before he'd turned, a good man. There were so many memories the two of them shared that she would love to relive. They'd been so happy together.

Would I be doing it for them, or for myself? She turned off the cold water and let her hair drip onto the shower floor. She stared at the tiled wall, dazed by her own will. She'd had razor focus for the last half-century. Find the book. Find the Coven. Slaughter them all. Slaughter herself. Now things were messy, and she had a choice in front of her she never expected.

She hadn't come to any decision about telling Julian by the time she stepped out of the shower and toweled off. Even without glancing at her phone, she knew Julian would have answered in the affirmative that she could come over.

Ellie cringed at the memory of running out of his place the night before. That probably hadn't been the best move, but she could admit now that she'd been shocked and scared by what she'd seen. It had been totally unexpected, and she didn't know how anyone else would have handled it better.

On the off chance it would trigger a memory, Ellie carefully selected her outfit, choosing something that was similar to what she wore when she and Max lived together. The floor-length dress was vintage and a bit more modern than what she used to wear, but she couldn't find anything better. Still, it was a lovely dress and she felt pretty wearing it.

She'd given up on her underwear and chose the least stretched-out ones she'd found. She hadn't dressed for the male gaze in years and now she was regretting it a bit. To her surprise, Ellie found she wanted to dress up for Julian.

The walk to Julian's was over in a flash. She'd been distracted, but she hadn't even been bothered by anyone on her way over, giving her no break from her own thoughts. When she finally reached his place, she knocked once before opening the unlocked door.

He must have been waiting for her because he jumped from the couch and rushed over to her as she closed the door behind her and locked it. Really, anyone could have gotten in. He probably should stop leaving it unlocked, even if it was just for her. He'd promised he kept it locked at all other times. The only reason it was unlocked when he knew she was coming over was so she could let herself in if he was upstairs. It was cute. He didn't approve of her walking around at night. If he knew the truth about her, he would never have to worry again.

"Are you okay?" Julian asked, raking her body with his eyes. He didn't comment on her dress, but she could tell that he liked it. Good. It had been for him.

Surprised, Ellie nodded. "I'm fine. Why?"

Shifting from one foot to the other, he asked, "You aren't upset about what happened yesterday?"

It clicked. He thought she'd run away the night before because something had been wrong. He didn't realize it was because she was overwhelmed and unable to process what had just happened. "No, why would I be?"

"You left in a hurry. I wasn't sure if it was because of something I did or..." He trailed off.

Ellie opened her mouth and then closed it, trying to think of a response. Finally, she settled on, "It was a lot, and I needed some time to process what we did and what it means. I'm fine now, I promise." She gave him a warm smile, hoping he'd take her words at face value. She couldn't explain the real reason she left, and she didn't want to lie to him. Doing so by omission was bad enough.

He nodded and she watched him visibly relax. The small smile he gave her was so similar to one Max used to shoot her in their private moments that she froze for a second. It was odd, seeing Max's mannerisms on someone else. Someone who didn't even know what they were doing. Or did he? How much of him was Julian and how much of him was Max?

"I wasn't sure I'd see you again," he admitted, bashfully rubbing the back of his neck. "I was hopeful, though. And hope—"

"Dies last," she finished for him.

He perked up with a chuckle. "Yeah, exactly."

The uncommon phrase Max had said to her so many times over the years warmed her from the inside out. Julian made her feel closer to those old memories.

"Care for a drink?" Julian asked, turning back to the kitchen. He had a steaming mug on the end table by where he'd been sitting, and she knew it was filled with hot chocolate. The man was addicted to it.

Disgustingly sweet.

"Sure," she said, following him.

With careful movements, he went about boiling water for a pot of tea in the delicate teapot he'd picked up just for her use. He'd picked up her favorite tea a while ago and had become quite adept at making it just the way she like it. If it was too strong, she was able to almost taste it. More than the taste, it was comforting to have a warm drink in her hands sometimes. There was something soothing about the simple sensation.

"You're staring," he said with his back still turned toward her.

Ellie chuckled softly. "Do you have eyes in the back of your head or something?"

He laughed, soft and low. "My mother used to do that all the time to me when I was younger. I was convinced for several years that she actually did have eyes in the back of her head." After a pause, he added, "She did nothing to dissuade me from the notion."

With a flourish, he turned around with the teapot and a cup in his hands. He walked past her and set them on the table to brew.

"I don't know how you can drink that stuff that strong," he grumbled, turning back to Ellie. "It's painful. It tastes like toxic sludge, I swear. Might as well eat potpourri."

She laughed. When she'd lived with Max, she'd had the same habit of drinking exceptionally strong tea to try to taste it. It was something of her humanity that she was hesitant to give up. Most of the time she forgot she'd ever been human, but occasionally small things would poke through, reminding her she'd once been different. Tea was one of those things for her. It was so little and so small that she'd never bothered breaking the habit. There was no hurt in doing so. In fact, she could argue it was good for her.

Staring at Julian, who was smiling wide at her, she wondered how she'd ever missed the similarities between him and Max. There were so many small mannerisms that the two shared. Sure, she could chalk them up to coincidence, but after reading Rodriquez's book, she wasn't so sure. Coupled with the memory he shouldn't have had, it was enough for Ellie to seriously consider whether Max had been reincarnated as Julian. It sounded crazy, and she was only half convinced, but the possibility seemed real and the hope she felt definitely was.

"You're staring again." Julian laughed and poked her in the forehead. "It's a bit creepy."

She laughed and rolled her eyes. "Kiss me."

The look of surprise on Julian's face only lasted a moment before he obliged and leaned down and kissed her, his lips soft and warm against her chilled ones. For half a second, she wondered how Julian excused away the fact she was always chilled. He'd never commented on it before, so perhaps she wasn't as cold to the touch as she thought she was.

She closed the distance between them and pushed her body against his, trying to get as close to him as possible.

Wrapping an arm around her and securing her, Julian seemed to have the same idea. They deepened the kiss, and Ellie sighed with contentment. After a moment, they broke apart and Julian released her only to grab her hand and pull her after him.

"We're going to make it to the bed this time," he told her, a smile playing on his lips. "Last time was nice but it was a bit cramped."

Although she'd enjoyed the last time on the couch, it had limited their movements and she was more than happy to experience sex on a bed with him. "Lead the way."

When they got to his room, he immediately pulled the shirt he was wearing over his head. "Take it off," he told her, staring pointedly at her dress.

With a coy smile, she lifted the hem of her dress and drew it over her head, leaving her in just the serviceable underwear she'd determined was the least ratty of her collection. Julian seemed more interested in everything else she bore rather than her underwear.

"You're beautiful," he muttered, ripping his pants down his legs. Ellie could already see the effect she was having on him through his boxers.

She stripped until she was completely naked and watched as Julian took her in. There was a desire in his eyes that mirrored that of Max's, and for half a second, she saw Max standing before her, not Julian.

"On the bed," he directed, pointing at his king-sized bed.

Obliging, she scooted to the center of the bed before allowing her legs to fall open. Julian stared as he stalked toward her, his eyes on her glistening core. Once he was on the bed, he gave her a wicked look before sliding between her legs.

Julian took his time, leaving soft kisses up her legs and following them with gentle fingers. He caressed her flesh before settling between her thighs and kissing her everywhere but where she really wanted. Ellie groaned in appreciation, remembering how Max used to do the same thing.

"Stop teasing," she grated through clenched teeth.

Julian obliged. He tasted her, and she let tense muscles ease into the mattress with a dreamy sigh.

Julian pinched with his teeth, just hard enough to mix pleasure and pain together. It was something that only Max had ever done to her, and she tugged on the back of Julian's head, gently gripping his hair and lifting his face so she could look him in the eyes.

"How'd you know to do that?" she hissed, searching his face for any recognition.

Confused, he stared at her. "I don't know. It just seemed like the right thing to do. I didn't hurt you, did I?"

Ellie shook her head.

"Then it was a lucky guess," he said, smiling at her. He dove back between her thighs, starting his worshiping all over again.

Staring at the ceiling, her eyes half closed, Ellie realized she truly believed he was Max. Somehow, he had come back to her. The only issue now was finding a way to make him remember.

CHAPTER THIRTEEN

Ellie lay in her bed, staring up at the ceiling. It wasn't quite dawn and she couldn't fall asleep yet. Usually, as soon as it came close to dawn, she was out for the day, but ever since she'd learned about reincarnation, she'd had a hard time falling asleep, her mind too busy racing through the possibilities.

Despite Julian's pleas to stay with him, Ellie left before the sun rose every morning. There was no way for her to safely sleep at Julian's without letting him know first what she was. If he was to try to rouse her during the day, her instincts would take over and she could seriously injure him, if not kill him. No, it was better for her to sleep in her own bed, in her own locked apartment in the basement. There was no chance of her hurting anybody. Maybe someday there would be a point when she could sleep over at his house, but that was still far away. He didn't even know that vampires were real, much less that she was one.

After her careful observations, she was convinced that Julian was really Max. There was no way there were two men that made her feel like she did, or that they had so many similarities. It was impossible. And their shared phrase about hope and how it died last? In all her three hundred years since losing Max, she'd never heard someone else say it.

The only problem was, Julian had no idea he was both a reincarnated vampire and her past lover. That wasn't a conversation you could come back from, and she had a feeling Julian wouldn't just automatically believe her. He was too logical. It was part of what made him so interested in alchemy. There was a logic and a sense that went with the experiments. Telling him he was reincarnated with just anecdotal evidence wasn't going to be enough to convince him, although it might scare him away, which she didn't want. She knew he cared for her, but she wasn't sure his affection for her went as far as excusing away complete and utter craziness.

She figured the safest method was to try to jog his memory so he remembered the past on his own. Ellie had no idea if he'd been reincarnated before or if this was the first iteration, but she did know there was probably a gap in his memory from the late fifteen hundreds until about thirty years ago, give or take a few years. She would start with the time when they'd been alive together and work out from there if needed.

In her opinion, it might be beneficial for him to research the last time period they'd been together. After rising from bed, she went to her stacks of books and started pulling out anything that had to do with the 1500s, whether it was straight human history or vampire literature presented as fiction. By the time she was done, she had a good stack of about a dozen books to bring over the next day. It was going to be cumbersome getting them all over to his place, but Ellie could handle it.

With a yawn, she made her way back to bed, falling fast sleep. Now that she had a plan, she was much more relaxed.

When she woke, she got ready quickly, packed a good

portion of the books in her backpack, and grabbed the rest to hold in her arms. It wasn't that the books were too heavy. They were just awkward to hold.

Julian laughed when he opened the door and found her standing on his doorstep with a towering stack of books. "What's all this? Did you really walk all the way over here with all that?"

Ellie nodded, dropping the books onto the couch and then turning to her backpack to remove the books in there. "I found a couple books I think you should read, or at least take a look at. They aren't your usual alchemy books, but I still think you'll find them interesting."

"A couple?" He laughed again. "Ellie, there's almost a dozen books here! When do you think I'll have time to read all these with school going on?"

Ellie paused. She hadn't thought about that. Although objectively she knew he was working on his PhD, that was a daylight endeavor that she had no part of. Honestly, she had no idea how he stayed up all night with her and then also did school.

"You'll figure it out," she finally said, shooting him a smile. She knew that if she asked him to read something, he'd find the time to do so simply because she wanted him to. It was an easy trait to take advantage of, and she never wanted to do that, but this was important. This was about bringing Max back. He'd understand her little manipulation.

"I guess I can find some time to browse them," Julian said, a smile still on his lips. "Although I can't promise how long it'll take to get through all of these. There are quite a few, and I do technically have other responsibilities."

Ellie bounced over and kissed his cheek. "That's all I ask." She graced him with a smile, and he smiled back before bending down and kissing her gently. There was nothing sexual about the kiss. It was simply an acknowledgment of what they felt for each other, and it delighted her.

Over the next couple of days, they pored over the books she'd brought. Although very little alchemy was mentioned, Julian seemed fully engrossed in the books and Ellie was pleased. Something had to jog his memory. She just had to figure out what it was. Once she'd worked that out, she could supply him with whatever information he needed. The first step was always the hardest, and she braced for the disappointment that might come with him not remembering fast enough.

Although the books she'd brought over dealt with the world as they'd known it, Julian didn't seem to remember anything from reading them. It was only when she brought *The Story* back over that anything interesting happened. She hadn't found the time to finish reading it with everything that was going on, and she figured she'd take her time at Julian's to finish.

"Can I see that?" Julian asked, reaching over for the book one night. "I never got a chance to finish looking at it after you stole it from me."

Ellie stuck out her tongue at him but handed it over, open to a few pages before the portrait of her and Max. Julian flipped through the pages and paused when he got to the portrait. He frowned down at the page. "This looks like us," he said slowly, tracing the planes of both their faces. Before Ellie could press him further, he added, "Why did I think that? It can't be. Besides, I don't look anything like this man."

The confusion he felt was written all over his face, and for a second, Ellie didn't know what to do. She was caught off guard.

Floored, Ellie stood after a second and hurried over to him to gaze down at the drawing. "It does look like me. Why did you think this man looked like you?" she pushed, trying to get him to force through whatever was blocking his memory. This was the first time he'd shown any interest in the portrait, and Ellie wondered if he'd just never seen it before or if something had changed to allow him to recognize them.

"I don't know. When I see this, I see us, but I'm darker than this man. He looks blond and has totally different features." To Ellie's disappointment, Julian shrugged. "I must just be tired." He turned the page, but Ellie couldn't help but feel like he was more affected by the portrait than he was letting on.

Disappointed, she sat back down and picked up another book. She felt like they had been so close and yet hadn't reached the finish line. Was Julian blocking the memories on his own, or was there some sort of cosmic gate in him keeping the past at bay? Ellie took it as a win that he'd recognized himself as Max, even if he didn't understand it. At least that was a start.

The next night, they were in the library again, poring over two new additions to Julian's collection, when Ellie heard him whispering in perfect Spanish. She whipped her head around and stared at Julian, who was tracing the inscription under a picture in the book he was reading.

"Did you just speak Spanish?"

Julian turned to her, a frown on his face. He glanced at the book he was reading and seemed surprised to find Spanish words staring back at him. "Did I? I was just reading the inscription. I thought… well it didn't look like Spanish to me, I guess. You know my Spanish isn't very good."

That was an understatement. His Spanish was absolutely terrible the few times he'd tried to talk to her. It had been endearing if a bit grating to the ears. They'd quickly decided he shouldn't try to speak in Spanish unless he was positive he knew what he was saying.

"Did you understand what it was saying?" she asked, trying to keep the excitement from her voice. This was progress. Max had lived with her in Spain. They'd both spoken perfect Spanish.

"I guess so. That's weird." He shrugged, brushing off the

strange occurrence. "Must have been from the recesses of my brain. Language is weird like that sometimes."

She stared at him, annoyed. Clearly this was Max breaking through, but Julian seemed content to just excuse it away. "You seem to be full of strange occurrences lately," she said. She tried to remind herself that Julian wasn't even aware he was withholding memories. It wasn't like he was doing this on purpose.

Julian looked up at her, a thoughtful expression on his face. "I guess." He frowned. "Actually, you're right."

For half a moment, Ellie felt bad for having said anything at all. Julian looked more and more distressed as he considered the several events that had seemed off in the past couple of days. She hadn't meant to upset him, but she felt he needed to be aware on some level that there was something going on. Coming out and saying it wasn't advisable, so she had to push the only way she knew how.

She knew for a fact that Julian was Max reincarnated. There were just too many things for them all to be coincidences. Over the next couple of days, she realized Julian was becoming more and more distressed and confused whenever she confronted him with something Max did that he also did. When she pointed these out or when she asked why he was doing something, he always seemed lost, as if she were speaking in riddles just to annoy him. It wasn't her intention to upset him, but she didn't know how else to get her point across without coming out and saying he was her reincarnated lover.

During the early mornings before the sun rose, she allowed herself to ponder whether she was doing the right thing by trying to get Max back. What happened to Julian if she was successful? Would the two personalities war with each other, or would Max completely take over? She adored Julian, but she missed Max. She couldn't decide which option would be the better of the two.

It was a thought that plagued her, but she pushed it aside. If there was any chance that she'd get Max back, she had to try, no matter the consequences.

She'd promised him forever, and that was what she was going to give him.

CHAPTER FOURTEEN

Part of Ellie had believed that as soon as she got Julian to remember one thing, everything else would fall into place. She felt certain that this rediscovery of his past self might come back to him the way memories did to an amnesia patient. Surely, once all the puzzle pieces found their places, Julian would look at her through Max's eyes, and she could tell him she did as he asked. She ran that night, and now here they were, three hundred years later, reunited.

She was bitterly disappointed to realize this was not the situation at all.

There were a few moments during their time together when Julian's gaze would suddenly seem far off, and he'd look lost. Ellie had the suspicion that these were moments where something of Max's life surfaced, and Julian was trying to process what he remembered. She didn't push him, only asking him what he was thinking so hard about.

Each time he'd shrugged and said, "Nothing," but Ellie knew better. If it had been anything else, Julian would have told her about it. The fact that he wasn't saying anything said more than he realized. She only wished that he would tell her what he was remembering. Were they flashes of a past life? Or were they memories of things he'd once done that he now did again?

She had so many questions and she didn't have anyone to ask. In a perfect world, she would still be in contact with Javier Rodriquez and would have been able to talk to him about the entire situation, but when Max had been murdered, she'd allowed the rest of her Coven to assume she'd been killed too. She'd never corrected them and actively avoided any place they might have been at. She was sure her memory was now long gone.

His reaction to the drawing was still the only indication that he remembered her or their past together, and as comforting as it had been at the time, over the next couple of days, Ellie began to resent that there wasn't more progress. She didn't expect Julian to remember everything overnight, but she did want him to remember something.

He had recognized his old body on some level even though he looked quite different now. That was progress even if it was only a small step. Maybe someday he'd look at that portrait and see himself.

Every morning she'd gone home frustrated with Julian having no clue. She wasn't trying to be unpleasant, but her patience was limited at best and at worst, nonexistent. She knew if it wasn't so important, she would care significantly less, and that was a hard pill to swallow. She didn't know what else she could do to help make him remember their past and their love for each other. Julian's affection for her was lovely, but it wasn't the wild love she'd shared with Max.

Nevertheless, being with Julian made her feel like she wanted to start living again. She'd bought new clothes and found she didn't mind cleaning up her space a bit. Hell, she had even bought her own teapot and kettle for her kitchen, meaning she had something in it. A sampler box of tea had caught her eye when she was in the store, and she'd bought that as well.

If anyone had told her she would have her very own teapot in her kitchen at some point, she would have laughed in their face. She wasn't here to live. She was here to exist.

But Julian was changing all that. He filled her nights with laughter and smiles and the acknowledgment that life didn't have to be painful and bad. It could have good moments as well, if one allowed it to. With Julian, she was beginning to accept that she didn't deserve to be in pain all the time, and that was scary. She'd been safe in her pain, and now she was being forced out of it and into the real world. It was scary and new, but she didn't regret it.

Why wasn't that enough for her?

She was going through her closet before bed one morning when she had an idea. In the back of her closet with the books that upset her, there were a couple of pages that might be enough to jog Julian's memory.

After her mad dash through the trees as she fled the vampire hunters, she'd spent several days wandering around the unknown forest she'd found herself in, feeding off any unlucky soul that crossed her path. She wasn't proud of the people she'd killed, but her instinctive will to live made her do it.

She'd been as close to feral as she'd ever been, her body still tuned to survival at all costs. When a vampire was woken up in the middle of the day, they ran off pure instinct, and Ellie felt like she'd done the same the first couple of days alone. She didn't remember much of it, and she didn't know if that was because she didn't want to or because the memory was gone. Regardless of the reason, she knew it was probably the darkest time of her life. The only time that was potentially darker were those moments she'd watched Max be murdered.

Once she finally regained some form of cognitive processes, she had slowly trekked back to the house she'd shared with Max. It had taken almost two weeks to find her way back. Part of that had been that she'd fled quite a distance in her mad rush, but the rest of it was that she had to avoid anyone who might recognize her. She couldn't trust anyone, especially those she'd once called family. They'd turned their backs on her and Max.

She remembered the house being on fire when they'd fled, but she had assumed someone would have put out the fire. Their house had been a beautiful manor, and she'd assumed someone would have wanted to save it and live there. To her surprise, there was little left but ash when she arrived. Standing where the front entryway had once been, she had stared at the rubble, her eyes seeing what once had been there.

Tears had threatened for the first time in days, but she'd pushed them back. There was no point in crying over a burned house when Max was gone. If he'd been here, he would have made some joke that would have made her feel better.

He wasn't there and the joke was never told, but she felt better at the thought. Max had wanted her to live, and she wasn't going to let some ruined manor stop her.

Despite this thought, she'd spent hours searching for anything that might have survived. She didn't have anything specific she was looking for. She'd just wanted to find something to take with her as proof that they'd once shared a life together.

Besides finding a hair clip and a brass button from one of Max's jackets, she'd given up on finding anything significant. Even still, she'd tucked both finds into her pocket, determined to keep them close.

She was in what used to be Max's study when something caught her eye. Walking over to the flapping paper, she found a few pages from Max's journal. To her surprise, she'd chuckled. The sound had been strangled and not quite right, but it was still something resembling a laugh. Of course, the only pages of Max's journals that had survived were these ones. She'd had no idea what the pages said as they'd been written in a code he'd created. Time and again, she'd joked with him about his secret language, but he'd never gotten around to teaching her the code, and now it was too late. Whatever brilliance he'd written down was lost forever.

Nowadays the originals were in a lockbox in Europe, but Ellie still carried this copy of a copy. Sometimes she still pulled it out and inspected the code, wondering if this was the time she would finally break it. It never was, and she always put the pages back disappointed.

If anything was going to help Julian to remember his past life as Max, it would be the presentation of his old work. At least, that was what she hoped as she made her way to Julian's house, the pages tucked safely in her backpack. This was the best plan she'd come up with, and she prayed it would help him remember something.

She couldn't stay in limbo like this forever. Even in her human days, she had never felt a draining fatigue like this one. This was not exhaustion of the body, but exhaustion of the heart.

When Julian greeted her at the door, she noticed the sunken skin below his eyes and the drawn way his lips curled in a smile. Their interesting schedule had never bothered him before, and Ellie wondered how much stress his body was under as his brain tried to remember the past. He looked about as tired as her heart felt, and she'd never considered the possibility that there would be a physical toll on his body. She'd assumed everything would be mental, but looking at him, she knew that wasn't the case. Every day he seemed more worn down, and Ellie wondered what his breaking point would be. She prayed they never got to that point.

He might not say anything about it, but she knew he knew something wasn't right. On some level, she hoped he just thought he was getting sick. They could make excuses for that, and his tiredness could be a symptom. Part of her was sure he knew the answer wasn't that simple. Julian was a smart man who seemed very aware of himself. He had to know that something else was going on and it wasn't a simple cold.

She smiled up at him. "I have a surprise for you," she blurted out.

Julian's eyes lit up. The last time she'd had a surprise for him, she'd shown him her new lingerie. It was black and lacy, and he'd thoroughly enjoyed taking it off her. He'd been like a kid at Christmas. To be honest, she'd enjoyed it almost as much as he did. She felt beautiful and sexy when he looked at her like that, and it was an addictive feeling.

"Not like that." She chuckled, moving toward the stairs. When they got to the library, she set her backpack on the desk and pulled out the sheets of paper. She gave them one more inspection before she handed them over to Julian.

Ever the academic, Julian's eyes lit up. "What's this?"

"Just read them. I think you'll be interested in what they have to say," she said, trying not to sound too excited.

He scanned the pages, one after the other, and Ellie realized he was actually reading them, somehow remembering and deciphering the code all at once. She consciously tried to control her body and stop herself from jumping up and down in excitement. He had no idea how big this was.

"This is incredible. It's an old alchemy recipe, or at least part of one. I've never seen anything this detailed before. It's incredible. Where'd you find it?" Julian looked over at her, his excitement mirroring her own.

Ellie couldn't stop the smile from spreading across her face. "You can read it?" she asked, ignoring his questions. She wasn't one to allow for misunderstandings. She wanted him to say it.

He glanced over at her with a puzzled expression and then turned back to the sheet. She watched the realization dawn that the recipe wasn't in English. "I didn't even realize this was in… code? How the hell did I read that?" he muttered more to himself than to Ellie. "That's definitely not English. Or any language I'm familiar with," he added.

"I know," she said, the glee clear in her voice.

"Is this like the Spanish caption?" Julian muttered. She could tell he was grasping at straws and was trying to make his sudden knowledge make sense, but he couldn't. He was an intensely logical man, and nothing about this made logical sense.

Julian turned back to Ellie, about to ask her something else, when she stood up on her toes and kissed him squarely on the mouth. Any doubt she might have had that Julian wasn't Max was gone. Only Max could read his own code. He'd never shared it with anyone, even her. For Julian to read the papers meant he was Max somewhere deep within him.

Her emotions were all over the place, but she knew she needed to be as close to him as possible. She needed him.

CHAPTER FIFTEEN

Whatever confusion Julian may have had about being able to read the notes was replaced almost instantly by desire. He grabbed her hips and pulled her flush against him, deepening their kiss until Ellie couldn't think straight anymore. There was an urgency to this kiss that wasn't always there, and she responded equally to it.

He pulled away just enough to rain kisses down the side of her throat, nippingly lightly as he went. She moved her head to the side, giving him better access. Her skin wouldn't bruise—her heart wasn't beating, after all—but she knew if she'd still been human there'd be a line of them going down her neck the next day.

With one smooth motion, he raised the edge of her shirt and separated from her mouth long enough to pull it over her head, revealing the lace bra he'd liked so much the other day. He growled in appreciation and cupped one breast through the fabric.

Max's hands had always been rough from working in the lab and around their manor, but as an academic, Julian's hands were soft, perhaps softer than her own. They danced across her skin, leaving a heated trail in their wake.

"Have I told you how amazing you look?" he whispered in her ear as his other hand dove beneath the cup of the bra and tweaked her nipple.

Ellie gasped, her senses going wild. She couldn't form any words as his other hand released her breast and went behind her to undo her bra. Once the band was released, she helped him push the straps down her arms and away from her, her bra falling to the floor. She couldn't take it off quickly enough.

Julian tore her jeans off, followed by her underwear. "Sit on the desk."

Ellie obeyed and was rewarded with Julian's mouth on her pert nipple. He rolled it with his tongue and then nipped it lightly with his teeth, sending a shock of sparks through her straight to her core. She moaned as he did it again and again, giving her no peace in between the sensations.

Once he was done with one nipple, he turned his attention to the other one and started it all over again. By the time he was finished, Ellie was a panting mess with no coherent thoughts in her head. All she knew was she loved the way Julian touched her, and she needed him to continue doing it, or else she would explode from need.

He smirked, knowing exactly what he'd done, and took off his shirt. He closed in on her again, forcing her to shimmy backward. Books, pens, and a heavy stone paperweight fell to the floor.

"You still have pants on," she pouted. It had just occurred to her that she was naked and he wasn't, which was so unfair. She wanted to admire him as well. Although he was leaner than Max had been, his body was just as built.

Julian laughed and unbuttoned his pants, letting them fall to the floor. He stepped out of them, and Ellie's gaze transfixed on the front of his boxers. He strained to be free of the confines of the fabric. She felt powerful knowing she could bring a man like Julian to such a state. She hadn't even touched him yet, not really.

Despite his protest, Ellie slid off the desk and pushed Julian toward it, perhaps a little too forcefully. He grunted as he was knocked up against it. More of his personal items tumbled to the floor. Something smashed.

"Sorry," she murmured, slipping her fingers under the waistband of his boxers, pulling them down, and setting him free.

She lowered herself to her knees and gazed up at him. Julian groaned in appreciation as she wrapped her lips around his hard length and took him into her mouth. One hand gripped the base of his shaft and the other cupped his balls lightly, applying just the slightest amount of pressure. As she started moving her head up and down, she took in more and more of him until he was hitting the back of her throat with every intake. She reveled in the clean taste of his skin, and she wondered how she'd gone decades without this.

Julian gripped her hair, stopping her movements. Ever so slowly, as if he were asking permission, he thrust into her mouth only a little at first. When she didn't complain, he did it again, this time going in more deeply.

There was something erotic about giving up control and allowing Julian to fuck her mouth. She relaxed into the sensation, not fighting him at all. The thrusts grew in ferocity until they were almost frantic, as if he couldn't quite believe his good luck and wanted to savor every moment of it.

To her surprise he didn't finish, instead, pulling all the way out. With his fingers still knotted in her hair, he guided her to her feet, turned her around, and bent her over the desk. This was new. Exciting. Ellie stretched to the tips of her toes, showing off the muscles in the back of her thighs and arching her back. Julian deserved a show. He let out a delicious growl of appreciation and gave her ass a firm slap. The sound echoed around the room, and she giggled coyly over her shoulder at him. Julian knelt and spread her open. He leaned forward and spread her slit with his tongue, licking her core.

Ellie's eyes almost rolled back in her head. She held on to a cry of pleasure and reached forward to grip the far edge of the desk for support. She gripped the wood so hard it bent and almost splintered beneath her fingers. She released it as her thighs began to tremble and Julian became bolder behind her.

He pressed two fingers inside of her. She bit down on her bottom lip hard enough to draw blood. *Yes.* He pushed down against her G spot, and every movement of his fingers brought her closer to the edge of ecstasy.

"*Julian*," she breathed. "Don't stop."

He didn't. He rose to his feet and held her up with an arm under her waist. He kept going until the world tipped and spun and her release broke her. Ellie strained to stay on her feet as her muscles quivered with the aftershock.

He wedged his knee between her thighs.

She spread her legs. "That's it," he purred. "Just like that."

She groaned when she felt his swollen, wet head at her entrance. In one smooth motion, he pushed into her up to his hilt, leaving no question of who owned who. Her senses were going wild with the rough wood of the desk on her nipples and the wondrous sensation of Julian filling her up. It was almost too much.

He pulled out so slowly that she nearly cursed at him for being such a cruel tease before pounding back into her. She wiggled her ass to adjust the depth, and he sank a little more into her, both of them moaning at the sudden change of angle.

Gripping her hips so hard she knew she would have had fingerprint-shaped bruises had she been human, he pounded into her, creating a steady rhythm that instantly brought her to dizzying heights. He edged her, almost letting her climax and then pulling her back from it again and again until she felt wild with need.

Finally, he rocked into her again, letting her crash over the edge. As her orgasm washed through her he yelled, "Eleonor!" as he came.

"Julian," she answered, her mind on the unending waves of pleasure that were washing over her. She didn't even realize at first that he'd called her by her first name.

Julian froze, his cock still twitching deep within her. "What? Who's Julian?"

Finally realizing what he'd said, Ellie froze as well.

Before she could answer, Julian said, "Julian. *I'm* Julian," more to himself than to her. His brow furrowed and he pressed a hand to his forehead. "Aren't I? Wait… no, I'm Max." He pulled out of her body and Ellie felt empty.

Standing up from her position on the desk, she turned to him. "Are you okay?" she asked, figuring it was probably the safest question to ask.

Julian stared at her, confusion written all over his face. He opened his mouth and then closed it.

"You said your name was Max. Do you know who that is?" she pressed, trying not to overwhelm him all at once. She tried to keep her excitement under control as it mixed with the pulsing pleasure still coursing through her.

He stared at her, but his eyes were far away. She knew he wasn't really seeing her even though she stood before him. Whether he was seeing Max's memories or something else entirely, she wasn't sure.

"Julian?"

His gaze snapped back to her, and he shook his head. "My name is Julian, right?" Before she could respond, he nodded. "Yes, I'm Julian. And you're Ellie." His brow furrowed. "Why did I say Eleonor?"

She felt a primal urge to tell him who and what she really was.

He can't handle it yet. Soon. But not yet.

She swallowed the truth. "I don't know. Do you know an Eleonor?"

Julian gave her a hard look. "Of course not. I would never call you someone else's name during sex." He paused. "Oh shit, I did just that, didn't I?"

"It's fine," she said, trying to calm him down.

"You seem awfully calm about me calling you someone else's name," he continued. "I'd be pissed if you did that while we were together."

"It's similar?" Ellie tried, not sure what to say that wasn't the truth. "Really, it's not a big deal."

"It is!" Julian hissed before pressing his hand to the side of his head. He looked awfully pale all of a sudden.

She straightened, her gaze fixed on his face. "Are you okay?"

Julian hissed in pain again, this time bringing his other hand up to his head. Before either of them could do anything, he collapsed onto the floor, letting out a startled cry of pain that made every fiber of Ellie's being scream with alarm.

"Julian!" Ellie dropped to the floor next to him. "What's wrong?"

"My head," he choked out.

She stared at him in horror. Whatever was happening right then, she was sure it was related to the memories he'd just experienced. What must it be like on a human mind to have two versions of one's self crash together? Why hadn't she thought to prepare for this?

"Let me help you up and we can get you to bed," Ellie said, trying to remain calm.

Julian gave no indication he'd heard her, but she pulled on his arm and helped him up. In his pain, he didn't seem to notice she was unnaturally strong, and she thanked the universe for small favors. He leaned heavily on her as they crept down the hallway.

When they got to the bedroom, he slipped into bed, groaning when his head hit the pillow. Ellie went to the bathroom and opened the medicine cabinet, searching for some kind of painkiller. Finding a bottle, she shook out a few and filled up the cup by the sink with water. She returned to Julian, and he took them without complaint.

She encouraged him to drink more water as beads of sweat appeared on his forehead. He was even paler than he had been downstairs. Her gut tightened. What had she done to him? The cup trembled in his hand, so she took it away and set it on the side table. He winced as he tried to get comfortable, and she reached out to stroke his damp hair away from his face.

"Hush, you'll be okay," she said softly. "Rest."

She stroked his hair until the tension eased out of him and he lost consciousness.

She felt like a fool. Of course, there was going to be a physical toll on him. She should have known better. She watched him sleep. Minutes faded into hours. She wished she could stay, but soon morning would break, and none of his windows were boarded. When he woke, he would discover what she was.

She had to leave.

"I'll come back," she promised as he slept.

CHAPTER SIXTEEN

Ellie threw the book she had been searching through across the room with more force than she had intended. It bounced off the wall with a thud, landing half open on the floor.

The entire room was strewn with books in various states of rejection. Normally, she treated every tome with the respect it deserved, but she was frantic and frustrated. It seemed that what she was searching for could not be found in any of her books written by vampires.

The situation with Julian—Max—seemed to be an anomaly, not the standard. She had figured as much but it was still frustrating not being able to find any information. Usually, she could find everything she was looking for and more.

With a sudden burst of energy fueled by her annoyance she grabbed her backpack and headed to Thoth's Bookstore. When she entered, she was surprised that no one seemed to be around. Normally, the eccentric owner was there to greet her and nod as she headed to the back. After a cursory glance around to make sure he was not about to jump out and frighten her as he had done occasionally, she closed the door behind her. The soft tinkling bell put her at ease.

Usually, Ellie would head straight back to the vampire section, but today she was looking for something different. Having never looked for the reincarnation section before, she had no idea where to start, but she would bet money that there was just such a section here somewhere. Thoth's Bookstore was known for their metaphysical and occult books.

After half an hour of wandering around, she sighed in annoyance. She'd always known the bookstore carried far more than just books on vampires, and her razor-sharp focus on acquiring as many of them as possible had been like wearing blinders. She'd missed so many other sections in her desperate search. In her quest to find reincarnation books, she passed half a dozen topics that, on any other day, she would be interested in browsing, but she did not have the time now.

Ellie smelled the girl stocking the shelves long before she came around the corner to discover her. Ellie blinked down at the small girl. Ellie could not even qualify her as a woman. She looked far too young to be in that category. She had thought that Mr. Grootu was the only one who worked at the store, and in all her nights here she had never seen another employee.

"Can I help you?" the girl asked, pausing her restocking. She gave Ellie a warm smile and blinked her long dark lashes up at her. The girl could have been anywhere between nine and thirteen. It was impossible to tell between the passing seconds, where her youthfulness seemed to shift and dance between the range.

"I'm looking for anything on reincarnation, true cases if at all possible." She hoped she didn't sound too crazy. "Not fiction."

The girl nodded as if she heard this all the time. Her dark curls bounced across her dainty shoulders. "You're almost there. Two rows over, third shelf on the left."

"Thanks." Following the directions, Ellie found herself in front of an entire shelf filled with books on reincarnation. After a thorough perusal, she selected the best five she could find. There were several others that looked like they had potential, but she figured it would be best if she did not overload herself right away.

After making her way to the front counter, the same girl checked her out and Ellie wondered briefly if she was related to Mr. Grootu.

"I am," the girl said as Ellie was grabbing the bag of books she had purchased.

"You are what?"

"Related to Mr. Grootu."

"Oh," Ellie replied, bewildered. Had she spoken out loud or were her thoughts just loud enough for the girl to hear? With an awkward wave, Ellie hurried out. A mystery to be solved another day, perhaps.

Once home, she spent hours poring over the books she had found. They were all firsthand accounts of reincarnations, but they were all so different. There didn't seem to be a common theme between them, which was what she needed. If she could figure out what made someone reincarnate, she might be able to figure out how to make Julian remember his past life—and keep him from suffering too much in the process.

Despite spending hours reading and rereading the books, she could not point to one single event that they had all experienced. It seemed reincarnation was even more fickle than she had assumed.

Much to her old laptop's despair, she searched the internet for any accounts of reincarnation, ending up on some seedy sites. Desperation clung to her, and no matter where she searched, she was not finding the answers she needed. She was not sure exactly what she was looking for, but she figured she would know once she saw it.

She had to up the ante. It was time to conduct her own case studies.

SHE HATED TO ADMIT IT, but she was feeding nearly every night in an attempt to find a human who held another's memories. Javier Rodriquez had said it was rare but happened occasionally. For the first time, Ellie wondered if she had fed from someone like this before and just not realized it.

The thought made her sick to her stomach. If only she had known what she knew now, everything could be different. She continued to feed past the point of being full, desperate to find someone who had lived another life at some point. She felt gluttonous and greedy, but her determination only grew with every unsavory creep she drained.

After she finished draining her latest disappointment in a dark alley, a blinking neon sign across the street caught her eye. *Psychic. Past Life Readings.*

Ellie abandoned the corpse, crossed the quiet street, and knocked on the door. When no one answered, she knocked a bit harder.

Finally, the door opened and a small woman, smaller even than Ellie herself, appeared. "I'm about to close," she said, giving Ellie a onceover. Her eyes grew round, and Ellie wondered what she saw.

Did she know Ellie wasn't human? Even worse, did she know she was a vampire?

Before Ellie could say anything to put the woman at ease, the psychic swallowed and said, "I guess I can stay open a little later for you. Come in, come in. Please wipe your feet."

Ellie fought the urge to ask, *What, you didn't see me coming?*

Ellie did as she was told, only stepping into the shop after she'd wiped her feet on the brightly colored rug that seemed out of place. It was a small place with only a table and two chairs populating the room. Despite this, there was an aura in the room that nearly vibrated with Ellie's arrival. For the first time since Ellie had seen the flashing sign, she knew she had found a real psychic. The thought both thrilled and terrified her.

"Please, take a seat, Ellie," the psychic said, sitting down in her own chair.

Settling herself down, Ellie did not comment on how the psychic knew her name without an introduction, and she was glad she hadn't made the sarcastic comment when she first came inside. Something about this place, and the odd old woman, felt right.

"I have an idea of why you're here," the woman said, "but I would like you to tell me in your own words. There's a different power present in that." She folded her hands and waited patiently for Ellie to start.

Ellie observed the woman. She looked uncomfortable and like she would rather be any other place, but Ellie did not sense any fear from her, only an overwhelming discomfort. It was similar to how she had felt back in the Coven when a traveling vampire of great renown had visited, and her father had made her sit for hours with them while they talked nonsense.

"It's a little complicated," Ellie started. "A long time ago the love of my life died. He was murdered before my eyes. I thought he was gone forever, and I must admit I haven't been dealing with his death well. I recently met a man, and he reminded me so much of my lost love. It was small things at first, but as we've gotten to know each other, the small things have added up. I've come to the realization that he's actually my lost love reincarnated, but I don't know how to make him remember the time we shared before." Ellie finished with a frown.

The psychic paled. "Is this man like you, or is he human?"

Ellie stared at her. The woman knew exactly what she was. After a moment, she answered, "Human," wondering if it really made a difference.

Sighing, the psychic laid her hands palms up on the table. Ellie followed the curves of the psychic's palms, wondering what secrets they held.

"The human psyche is a delicate thing," the woman said. "It may seem robust, but in truth, it is nothing but a fragile flower. One wrong move and it can be destroyed forever. While reincarnation is a natural occurrence for some individuals, those that come back are never meant to remember their past lives. They are sealed away inside themselves. Sometimes something breaks through, but it's never for long and the individuals often don't even notice."

"Why not? It's still them, isn't it? If their past selves are still them, why can't they remember? That seems terribly unfair."

"Unfair to this human man of yours, or unfair to you?"

Ellie considered flashing her fangs. She came for a particular set of answers, not a character assessment. Instead, she shifted her position. "What else can you tell me?"

"The occasional glimpse of feelings one may experience from a past memory are only meant to guide us in our current lives. When someone dies, regardless of if they are reincarnated, they are dead in a sense. A separation occurs between who they once were and who they are now. Think of it like the Grand Canyon. You may be able to see the other side, but even yelling across it is impossible. Everything gets lost in the middle. Trying to force someone to remember a past life could cause grave damage to the individual—perhaps even death. There isn't much research on it since it's such a rare occurrence, but what is known highly recommends no one try to remember a past life."

Ellie stared at the psychic, trying to process her words. "So, you're saying I shouldn't even try?"

The woman shook her head. "It's best if you don't." She glanced at her watch, then around her barely decorated room as if searching for something. "I really was supposed to close before you came in. There's nothing more I can do for you. If you don't mind." She gestured toward the door.

Knowing she was making the woman uncomfortable, Ellie nodded and rose from the table. She passed the woman a twenty-dollar bill before making her way back out into the night. Her mind was going a million miles a minute. She didn't want to believe the psychic, but she'd witnessed firsthand the pain Julian had been in when he'd had that flash of memory. That entire situation had been him remembering on his own. But what would happen if Ellie tried to force him to remember?

How could she keep trying to get him to remember when it was causing him pain? Even worse, what if the psychic was right and making him remember actually killed him?

How would she ever be able to live with herself after that?

CHAPTER SEVENTEEN

While she had been researching reincarnation, Ellie had kept her distance from Julian. She had replied to his messages but had declined all invitations to go to his house. He did not press her. The last time she had cut him from her life, he had tried to get in contact with her for weeks. This time was different, though. Checking her phone to get the time, Ellie saw there were no missed calls or messages from him.

On her way home from the psychic, Ellie tried to calm her racing thoughts. She had wanted information on reincarnation, and she couldn't be mad just because what she found was not what she wanted to hear. Even the books she had bought had not been able to provide as much information as the psychic had in less than twenty minutes.

Ellie wanted to be shocked by what she had learned, but a small part of her had always figured that there was something more going on. She didn't mean to be a pessimist, but her life had always been one big tragedy. Why would finding Max's reincarnated self be any different? Of course, she would have the misfortune of finding her lost love and then have to leave him all over again.

What concerned her most was how fragile the psychic had made Julian's psyche sound. Ellie had never given the mind much thought, but she had always assumed it was a sturdy thing. Life was filled with adversity and to get through it, one had to be strong. It had never occurred to her that the opposite was true.

But then again, how many ancient vampires lost their sense of time and their connection to people? It was a common occurrence, and very few of the oldest vampires were still mentally present all the time. The passage of time was hard on a mind. Remembering a past life seemed like just the type of thing to break someone's head.

Despite casting around for another solution, she came to the painful conclusion that she needed to stay away from Julian. If his psyche was as fragile as the psychic had said, there was a very real chance that she could cause lasting harm by simply being with him.

When they'd had sex, he had thought he was Max for a moment, and he had recognized her as Eleonor. Her very presence had been enough to bring back such a strong memory. The last thing she wanted to do was hurt Julian physically or mentally, but it seemed inevitable if she stuck around. She either needed to end it with him or take the risk of irrevocable harm and stay.

If she was more selfish, she would choose to stay and just deal with whatever happened to Julian. She had never been an evil person, but Max had always brought out the best in her, and that had not stopped with time.

The decision was an easy one to make. If Max had been reincarnated as Julian, it was because he had earned a happy, full, human life, something that had been stripped from him the last time he had been on this planet. No matter her feelings for him, she was not going to stand in his way. He deserved happiness, and she was going to facilitate it to the best of her abilities, even if she had to hurt him a little in the process.

The only silver lining was, although Ellie loved both Julian and Max, she could not determine if Julian felt the same way. He was definitely fond of her, but there was no proof that he loved her. This would be more painful for her than it would be for him, and she took a small bit of comfort in this. If she could make this painless for him, she would.

Unlike the last time she had left Julian, Ellie pulled out her phone and sent him a text. It was short and to the point and held no emotion whatsoever.

I think it's best we end this while we are ahead.

It was the coward's way out, but she didn't know what else to say. If she told him never to contact her again, she knew he would blow up her phone. As long as he thought she felt something for him, he would continue to pursue her. This casual, emotionless text was the best she could do.

She would not put it past him to find her apartment and appear at her door. The thought brought a small smile to her face. She had no idea what she would do in such a situation, but it was nice to imagine being wanted that much.

Turning her phone to silent so she wasn't tempted to text or call him if he replied, she continued her walk back. It was quiet, and after her excessive diet over the past few days, she was feeling uncomfortably full. She could not remember the last time she had fed every night, sometimes multiple times.

Entering her messy apartment, she dropped her bag with a sigh. She might as well clean up some. She wasn't a neat freak, but she did like her space in some sort of order, not that one could tell from its current condition. It was better to be occupied than idle, especially when her mind was so full. She had too much weighing on her and found that keeping her hands busy kept some of the thoughts at bay.

Julian's silence only affirmed her belief that he knew something was wrong. The last time she had disappeared, he'd called her daily trying to get her to talk to him. But this time, there was nothing. The only difference was that, the first time, he remembered nothing, and now he remembered something, however briefly. He had been in physical pain the last time she had seen him, and she had been the cause of it.

Maybe he was frightened of her.

Over the next couple of days, Ellie kept to herself, spending most of her nights wandering the city, careful not to stray too close to Julian's house.

After a week, she realized the city no longer interested her. On a whim, she started searching online for apartments in other big cities. No particular city drew her. She just knew she needed to leave New York City. She wasn't sure how long her self-control would last before her will broke and she inevitably ended up back at Julian's door, begging for his forgiveness.

The only requirement was that the city was large enough to hide her feedings. Small towns may have their charms but being accused of murder was not on her to-do list. She had spent hundreds of years avoiding just that and was not about to kill her record now.

The only thing keeping her away from Julian was knowing he was finally getting what he had always wanted as Max. When she and Max had been vampires together, they had dreamed of nothing more than being human again. Every passing decade just made them long for it even more. Ellie had been turned as a young girl, but Max had been an adult when he had been attacked. He still remembered what it was like to be a human man, whereas Ellie's memories grew foggy and muddled with time. Being a vampire had always hit Max harder than it hit her.

Ellie had accepted the reality that this dream was just that. Nothing they did or did not do would turn them human again. Being a vampire may not have been their choice, but it was all they had. Maybe she was more accepting because of the age at which she had been turned, or maybe it was simply her personality. Perhaps it had been both.

Max had not accepted this, though. He had always believed if he tried hard enough, he might be able to turn them back into humans. Ellie had been too kind to crush his hopes, despite her disbelief. She had let him imagine all types of scenarios that might work, but she had never gotten her own hopes up. Instead, she focused on building a life with him that they enjoyed.

Now, though, he was human again. He may not know that he had once been a vampire, but Ellie knew Max would have been delighted with the turn of events. She could not steal that away from him, even if she was the only one who would know she had.

At the end of the day, they couldn't be together, and staying in the city would only torment her. He was happy as Julian, and he deserved to live that life. She just wanted him to be happy.

With all her newfound free time, Ellie turned to *The Vampire Hunter's Handbook*. She found it morbid yet entertaining in a trainwreck kind of way. The creators had spent ages creating the book, and Ellie could tell. It was incredible in its own horrible way.

It turned out there were more ways to kill a vampire than she had realized. Beheading and burning were tame compared to some of the other options in the book. She found she could only stomach a few methods at a time before she had to put the book down.

Some of her personal favorites revolved around religion. Crosses and the like didn't do anything to vampires, so she had always thought the general idea of religion harming a vampire was ill-founded. Apparently not. Holy water had always been a slight irritant to the skin, but she had always assumed it would not cause any real damage. After reading the *Handbook*, she guessed this was technically still true, at least until you injected holy water into a vampire's veins. Then it was an extremely painful way to die from the inside out.

Feeding on a clergyman on holy ground was another way to die, although this seemed way less gruesome than some of the other options. Did the clergyman volunteer to test this or did the stars align for it to happen with a witness? Did the vampire even need to know it was holy ground? Ellie had several questions about this method and how it had come about in the first place, and to her disappointment, the book did not explain much beyond the method of death. It did note that death was quick enough for the vampire that the clergyman was more than likely to survive.

All the methods had detailed illustrations explaining the methodology, and Ellie was fascinated by the time and effort that must have gone into making the guide.

The worst image by far was the illustration of a vampire being doused in oil, having their appendages removed, and being burned to death. It was a combination of several other methods, and despite herself, Ellie found it rather interesting.

At one point in time, she would have started trying to complete the easier methods on herself. Death had been her goal for so long now it felt odd to realize her priorities had changed. She found she could not stand the thought of leaving a world in which Max existed even if they were separated by fate. Knowing he was breathing was enough for her.

CHAPTER EIGHTEEN

Ellie accepted the silence from Julian as her due, and for weeks, they had no contact. She placated herself with the knowledge this was how it was supposed to be. Once she moved, the temptation to show up on his doorstep and beg for forgiveness would dissipate and she would be left feeling like an empty shell again.

There was comfort in the familiarity of her pain. It would be lessened, of course, by knowing that Julian was back in New York City living his best human life.

Her phone rang, bringing her out of the post-feeding stupor she'd been riding since she got home from hunting. "Hello?" she answered, not even bothering to look at the caller ID. Only one person ever called her. If it had not been so close to dawn and she had not been so sleepy, she would not have answered the phone. This was probably a lie, though, and even she could acknowledge this.

"Ellie," Julian said, his voice a bit hoarse. He cleared his throat and added, "How are you?"

After swallowing down all the words she wished she could say, Ellie said, "Fine. And you?"

"Good. Good. You're probably getting ready for bed, aren't you?"

"I am." There were several moments of silence. Finally, Ellie asked, "Do you have class today?"

"Yeah. I have to be ready in a couple hours."

She had no idea what to say to this, so she made a noncommittal grunt. When it appeared Julian was willing to sit on the phone in silence forever, she asked, "What can I help you with, Julian?"

"I miss you."

Ellie opened her mouth and then closed it without saying a word. Finally, she decided on, "It's been a while." It was not a lie. It conveyed absolutely nothing, but it was not a lie.

"It has. Honestly, my house feels empty without you. It's amazing how quickly I became accustomed to your presence."

She grunted but did not respond.

"I want to work things out, Ellie. Please. I'm not ready to say goodbye to you. We barely even started, but even you have to admit how right this feels. It feels like fate. You have to feel it too, right?"

A quiet, "Julian," was all she could muster.

"You have to feel it too, Ellie. I know I'm not the only one. I know how you look at me. I know what I feel. I gave you space," he added, "as much as I could bear. But..."

Ellie sighed and closed her eyes.

"Come over, please."

"What if, no matter what you feel, we can't be together, Julian? What if it's not meant to be and there's nothing we can do to change it?"

"You can't believe that's true," he whispered.

Ellie didn't know how to respond. She didn't believe it, not really. She wanted to believe that, no matter what, she and Max would always find their way back to each other. But then the psychic's words came back to her, and she knew it was for the best that they were not together.

"Come over," Julian begged. "Please. Just tonight. Let's work our way through this. I know we can. There's no reason why we can't."

"We don't belong together," Ellie forced out through clenched teeth.

"Then if this is truly goodbye, I think I deserve this much. Come over and tell me you don't want me in person. I'll accept it then, but I refuse to accept it now."

"I don't know," Ellie said. "I don't know if this is a good idea." It was a horrible idea, and she knew it, but she was tempted all the same. Seeing Julian just one more time was enough temptation for her to consider going over.

Closure.

Did she even deserve that?

"Give me this, Ellie. I've never asked you for anything, but I'm asking you for this. Please."

She wanted to say no—really, she did—but she wasn't that strong. "Okay." Her voice sounded small even to her ears, and she wondered how Julian could hear her. She knew instantaneously that she was making a mistake, but she didn't care. This was what she had wanted when she picked up the phone—an excuse to see him one more time. She felt a pang of resentment toward her lack of will.

Letting out a sigh of relief, he asked, "Are you free now?"

Ellie glanced at the time and sighed. It was only half an hour before dawn. It would take her that long to get to his house. "I really need to sleep. I can come over tomorrow night first thing, though."

Julian was silent for a moment. "You really can't come over now?"

Ellie shook her head. "No, I really can't. But I promise to be over tomorrow."

"Okay. See you then."

They clicked off, and Ellie tossed her phone aside as she lay down, wrapping herself up in her blanket. She wished things were different and she could go over now, but she felt the light of dawn inching its way toward her. She'd be unconscious in minutes. Julian would have to wait.

The next night, Ellie was up as soon as the sun set.

After shooting Julian a quick text, letting him know she was on her way, Ellie locked her apartment behind her. She had nothing worth stealing unless one considered the books she had collected, but those were an acquired taste and not a prime target of thieves.

Taking her time on the walk over, she tried to order her thoughts into some semblance of sense. It would not do to arrive as a blubbering mess. She had already promised herself that she wasn't going to cry, no matter how upset she or Julian became. That would not help the situation and might confuse him. Hell, she was confused herself, and they had not even spoken yet.

No matter what Julian might think, she knew they were not getting back together, or as together as they ever had been. Could she even call what they'd had a relationship? They'd had sex and they had spent almost every night together, but they had never discussed what they were. As curious as she was about his thoughts on the matter, the time to ask had ended.

She resolved to tell him she was leaving the city for good when she saw him. The location was not important, as long as he understood she was leaving and not coming back no matter what. He could focus on his studies, and she… well, she could slip back into the darkness where she belonged.

Feeling better with some semblance of a plan, she sped up, anxious to get it over with. The sooner she got there, the sooner she could tell him and the sooner she could leave.

When she finally got to Julian's she rapped once, and the

door pushed open on its own. Dread coiled in the pit of her stomach. Julian had been known to leave the door unlocked for her but never open. They were in New York City, after all.

She'd pointed out time and again how dangerous it was for him to leave his door unlocked for her, and every time, he had laughed her off, saying there was no one in the area that would think of breaking in. No matter what she had said, he would not take the threat seriously. Had his trusting nature finally gotten him into trouble?

With careful silent steps, she entered, scanning the hallway for any signs of an intruder. For a moment, she considered calling out for Julian, but she disregarded the idea almost immediately. If there was an intruder in the house, she did not want to warn them of her presence. As a vampire and a predator, she was naturally silent, and she moved down the hallway without making a sound. If there was someone in the house, they would have no idea she was there.

Peeking around the corner into the front room, she found no one. Everything seemed to be in its place, which was a relief. It didn't look like Julian had been robbed. With each step through the room toward the kitchen, her confusion grew and grew. There were no indications that there was an intruder present, but that didn't explain the open door and lack of Julian.

As she approached the kitchen, the smell of blood wafted toward her. Ellie froze, fear coursing through her veins. Oh no. Bracing herself for anything, she peeked around the corner into the kitchen. It appeared empty, and after stepping into it, she found a bloodied knife sitting on the cutting board. The amount of blood present was minimal, and she assumed Julian must have nicked himself while he was cooking. For a brief, sharp moment, she considered swiping her finger through the blood and pressing it to her tongue.

She resisted.

She glanced around and found no evidence of a second

person. Taking the stairs two at a time, Ellie stopped before the library door, which was shut. Now that was unusual. The door was always open. She turned the handle, half expecting it to be locked for once. It was not, and she pushed the door open and stepped inside.

The sharp tang of fresh blood greeted her, and her eyes narrowed in on Julian. He was leaning on the desk, staring at her, his hands full with a cross and a plastic vial of what Ellie assumed was holy water. She had no clue where Julian had gotten either of these items, considering he was not religious. He had a small Band-Aid on his finger, indicating where the scent of blood was coming from.

As she stepped toward him, he raised the cross as if to ward her off. He didn't look like he feared her, but he definitely was not looking at her like he wanted to 'work things out' as he'd said on the phone.

He knows, she thought sharply. She wasn't sure how he'd riddled it out, but his gaze tracked her movements as if he expected her to turn into a bat or a creature of the night before his eyes and attack him.

With a snort, Ellie reached out and pushed the cross down. "That's a myth," she said. "Holy water, too, unless you plan on injecting me with it. If you really want to kill me, you'll need to use concentrated UV radiation, and I know for a fact you don't have any of that lying around."

He lowered his hands, and the cross slipped through his fingers. "Is it true?" Julian asked, his gaze fixed on her mouth, probably to see if her fangs were sticking out. She was relieved the smell of blood was faint. Otherwise, her fangs might have made an appearance of their own accord. He smelled delicious.

"Julian," she said slowly. How could she navigate this conversation? He already looked like a scared bird, staring at her with wide eyes. He'd lost a lot of sleep. His skin was pale. Had he shut himself up in this house all these weeks?

"Just tell me," he managed.

Ellie lifted her chin. "It's true."

He balked.

She eyed the cross and holy water skeptically. "What do you remember?"

CHAPTER NINETEEN

Julian stared at her for a long moment before collapsing back into the chair at his desk and running his hands through his hair in agitation. The gesture was so familiar that it sent an arrow of affection through Ellie. All she wanted to do was smooth out the mess he had made, but she resisted.

"I don't know," he said. "I remember so much, yet I feel like I've forgotten even more and it's just out of reach. I have no idea what's real anymore." He scrubbed at his face. "I was half convinced I was crazy. I mean, how can *vampires* be real?" He shot her a glance as if begging her to tell him they weren't real, but she couldn't do that.

Ellie leaned against the desk and rested her hand on his shoulder. He did not flinch away, and she considered it a win. "Why don't you start at the beginning and work forward from there? I might be able to help fill in some blanks. I was there for a good portion of it, after all."

He nodded and considered his hands for a moment before he started talking. "When I first saw you, I thought you looked familiar, but no matter how hard I tried, I couldn't place where

I'd seen you before. I thought at first, we might have had a class together at some point, but it became obvious quickly that wasn't the case. I chalked up my compulsion to get closer to you as me wanting to figure out where I knew you from, but I think I knew even then there was more to it. Heck, I hadn't even seen your face and I was drawn to you. When you turned to look at me the first time, I felt as if I'd been sucker punched, but I couldn't figure out what had caused it. I've seen lots of beautiful women, but you? You took my breath away.

"I was drawn to you from the moment I saw you. Sure, you were looking at a book I'd been interested in, but I just used that as an excuse to get close to you. You could have been reading a book I'd never heard of before and I still would have approached you. Honestly, you could have asked me to go to the moon and back that night and I would have done it for you without hesitation.

"That was the first night the dreams came." He shuddered as he spoke.

Ellie squeezed his shoulder in reassurance. "What dreams?"

Julian frowned. "That first night I went to sleep, and I woke up as a man living sometime during the 1500s. The clothing I was wearing was European, and I was traveling with a big group of men. Some of them had brought along families, but the majority of them seemed to be traveling alone. We were camping alongside the road one night when a figure came out of the trees and attacked. I can't say for a fact whether it was human or not. It was... terrifying to behold. I watched it throw a man twenty feet into a tree trunk, breaking his back instantly."

Ellie listened. She'd heard the story before.

"My companions and I tried our best to fight off the thing as we were all trained swordsmen, but it was too fast and too strong. I woke up just as it ripped out my throat and started drinking."

Julian shuddered, and Ellie did not blame him. Vampires

who did not take care of themselves often lost control and turned into wild beasts intent on killing. That was part of why being in a Coven was so important. There were others around to keep you accountable. A pang of longing shot through Ellie. She might have given up her Coven when she had been betrayed, but that didn't stop her from missing the closeness she had once felt.

Family.

She would never find such a thing again.

"I woke up and my heart was pounding out of my chest, and for a moment, I couldn't figure out why my heart was beating at all. I thought it was an odd thought at the time, but I chalked it up to being part of the nightmare. It didn't occur to me that I was remembering a time when my heart didn't beat anymore." He frowned at this, as though the words tasted odd on his tongue. "The dreams kept coming. They didn't happen every night, but they were often enough that I came to expect them."

"What were the other dreams about?" Ellie asked, curiosity getting the best of her.

Julian shrugged. "There was a lot of traveling. I have to admit, the views in the dreams were spectacular. Sometimes my heart would be beating in them, and sometimes it wouldn't, but there was never any rhyme or reason to it. After a while, I stopped noticing. After a while, I dreamt of a commune of sorts, of vampires like me who all lived together in harmony. An older man ran the place, and I think he made me nervous. There was a love of power present that made it seem as if he would give up everything to hold on to his position."

Ellie nodded. She knew he was speaking of her father, and he was right with his assessment of him. At the time, she had known that her father loved his position as leader of the Coven, but she had wrongly assumed he loved her more. That was what a father should do, at least. Maybe it was because he had only adopted her, or maybe it would have been the same whether she had been his biological child, but he chose the Coven over her life, and that was something she could never forgive him for.

"Nothing led me to believe that any of these dreams had anything to do with you until the first time we had sex." He gave Ellie a baleful glare. "I think you bit me."

Ellie tipped her chin in acknowledgment. "I did. I hope I didn't hurt you."

He shifted uncomfortably. "Well, that night when I... came," he said hesitantly, "for a single heartbeat, I wasn't me. I was the dream man, watching you come undone in a different bed in a different time period. I thought perhaps I hadn't been getting enough sleep and that's why the dream melded with reality. It only lasted for a moment, which helped me excuse it away, but after that, I couldn't help but make the connection between the dreams and you."

"Were any of the dreams about me?" Part of her hoped they had been. She was curious to see what he had remembered.

How Max had seen her.

Julian shook his head slowly. "No, not the dreams I had at night. If I had seen you, I might have realized that you were the key connecting everything. Looking back, I feel a bit silly having not realized that you were the common thread."

"If I wasn't in the dreams, how could I be the common thread?" Ellie asked, a bit confused.

"You weren't the common thread in the dreams. You were the common thread in real life. When you went away, the dreams slowly started fading. I had been experiencing them several times a week, but all of a sudden, I was only experiencing a half dream one day a week. On one hand, I was relieved that the dreams that unsettled me so much were over, but on the other hand, I was devastated because they'd felt so real to me. To be honest, I thought I might be going crazy. I spent a good portion of our time apart trying to right my sleep schedule. I even made an appointment with a psychiatrist, but I ended up canceling that. I felt too crazy and didn't want a professional to agree and lock me up. I didn't have the time to end up in a mental hospital, and I felt like that's where I would be placed if I opened up about what was happening."

"So what changed?"

Julian shrugged. "You'd left that note, the alchemy recipe? Despite not knowing how I could read it, I could read it, so I decided to try it out." He glanced toward a desk drawer, and Ellie figured that was where the copy of the paper was. For the thousandth time, she wished she had made Max teach her the code so she could read it on her own.

Ellie perked up. "Did it work?"

"It was a complete and utter failure." Julian snorted. "Absolutely terrible. I never plan on recreating it. The smell was terrible. I even had to throw out the clothing I'd been wearing. The damn thing exploded, and goop got everywhere. Took me hours to clean up. I really should have put a warning at the end of that one saying it was a disaster. But that's not the interesting part."

"Oh?" Ellie said, trying not to giggle at the image he had created. The explosion and aftermath certainly seemed like the interesting part to her.

"No. The interesting part was, right as the explosion happened, I blacked out and fell to the floor. Memories I couldn't place of me and you came flooding back. It was as if we'd shared another lifetime together. And then... well, then I remembered dying. I remember being in the carriage with you and the hopelessness I felt before I realized you could still move. I almost asked you to save me, but I knew if you tried, we would both die. I'm so happy you made it out, Eleonor. So, so happy."

Julian shuddered, and Ellie squeezed his shoulder.

He reached up and placed his hand over hers. "I realized then what happened when I came to. Everything suddenly made sense. I'm Max, Eleonor. I remember all the years we spent together. I fell in love with you as Max, and I fell in love with you as Julian. We were always meant to be together, and I want to be with you. I love you, whether you're Eleonor or Ellie or someone else entirely. I've spent the past couple of days trying to wrap my head around everything, but I get it now."

He stood and wrapped an arm around her waist, bringing her flush against him. "I am never letting you out of my sight again. We have spent far too much time apart, and I am fully prepared to correct this. If you let me, that is. I won't force my company on you. I'm not that selfish." He tilted his head to the side in consideration. "Actually, I take that back. I might just be that selfish."

Ellie stared up at him, terrified she had just made up the last few moments. This was everything she had ever wished for, and it seemed too good to be true. "Max?"

"Yeah?"

"What do you want me to call you?"

Julian opened his mouth and then closed it. "I guess whatever you want. It doesn't really matter to me."

"Julian, then," Ellie said, finding it was easier to call him this in his current body.

"As you wish." Lowering his head slowly, Julian pressed his lips to hers.

With a little coaxing, she opened her mouth, and Julian swept inside, taking control of the previously hesitant kiss. Arousal and bloodlust coursed through her, making her dizzy.

He kissed her like Julian and he kissed her like Max always had. He kissed her until her knees were weak and he was practically holding her up.

"Bite me. I want to remember everything, Ellie. Please."

That was all the encouragement she needed. Her bloodlust and her attraction to Julian had combined into a heady drug of its own. Her fangs had already extended, and she pulled away, only to return, sinking her teeth deep into his neck. The fresh taste of blood prickled her senses, and she drank deeply.

CHAPTER TWENTY

There were few things that brought Max as much joy as spending hours in his laboratory. He had designed the entire setup and had spent a ridiculous amount of money stocking it. There was something to be said about being a timeless being. You tended to collect wealth.

When he and Eleonor had moved into the manor, they'd converted the basement into his study and lab. Max spent hours every day down there, working away. Eleonor tended to leave him to it. He didn't think she really understood what he was doing, but that was fine. He knew and she supported him, and that was all he really wanted.

Usually, the only thing that could pull him out of the lab was his Eleonor. She had a way of sweeping down the staircase and taking all his attention away from whatever he had been working on.

"Max?"

"Hmm?" Max answered, his focus on the dropper he was using to drip rosehip oil into the potion he was stirring with the other hand. He had to add exactly eight and a half drops, or the entire potion would collapse in on itself. It was a delicate process and he had to get it right. There were no second chances with this one.

Eleonor waited for him to straighten. "How much longer are you going to be?" she asked. "It's only a few hours before dawn. You've been down here all night."

Max glanced at the clock and then at Eleonor. "Not much longer. Have you eaten yet?"

It had been her turn to go into town and find a victim, and he knew how she dreaded feeding days. Sometimes he thought if he did not remind her to eat, she would completely forgo it, which was dangerous.

She nodded, and Max noticed a sadness hanging around her. He walked over and gave her a quick kiss. "I won't be much longer, I promise. Go relax, and I'll find you when I'm done." Maybe by then she would have worked through whatever was weighing on her or at the very least be ready to talk to him about it.

"Okay," she sighed before turning and making her way up the stairs. Max watched her go until her skirts were gone from sight. For half a second, he considered abandoning his potions and following her, but he resisted the urge.

He knew he had been spending more time in his lab than usual, but it was unavoidable. Eleonor said she understood, but Max knew she did not. Part of that was his fault. He had not told her what he was up to down here. He did not want to keep it from her, but he knew he was so close. He just could not tell her until he had perfected it. Then he would tell her.

Then they would celebrate.

Max had several potions bubbling around him in the lab, all different iterations of the same recipe. He found making and testing in batches was much more efficient, as some of the ingredients had to stew for over twenty-four hours. When he had first started out, he had only been making a single batch at a time, but after he realized how often he was messing up, he had decided on batches.

He turned his focus back to the belladonna clippings on his table. Carefully, he stripped the stem and added the leaves to the closest potion. For a second, nothing happened, and then the potion smoked and turned a sickly shade of green. Max prayed this meant it was finally stable enough to be used. His problem so far had been both the instability of the potion and the intensity of it. The potion either did too much or not enough, and nothing in between.

Satisfied, Max removed the potion from the flame. As it cooled, he went to his cabinet and pulled out a vial of his own blood. It was thicker and darker than human blood and had the added benefit of being completely shelf-stable. No matter how long it was left out, it would not clot.

He had had to hide the vials from Eleonor's view when she visited him down here. If she knew he was pulling his own blood as samples, thus making him need to feed more often, she would be upset. He knew her concern for him came from a place of love, but he didn't want to upset her if it could be helped.

Besides, this was worth the sacrifice.

He returned to the potion and dipped a miniature ladle into the liquid, pulling out just enough for his test. With bated breath, he dropped a few drops of liquid into his blood and waited. For a moment, he thought he had finally figured out the cure. The potion sank slowly below the surface of his blood, which seemed a touch lighter in color. Then his blood began to curdle and violently smoke, making him drop the vial onto his worktable. He watched as the blood eventually disappeared, leaving a green goo at the bottom of the tube.

Max closed his eyes, frustration and anger boiling up inside him. He had been working on this particular recipe for the better part of the month, and he had thought he had finally cracked the code. The goal was to make a kind of poison, but not a poison powerful enough to kill.

He might have made a very powerful vampire poison, but that wasn't what he was going for. He was searching for a cure, dammit. A cure, not a poison. He did not want to be a vampire, just as Eleonor wished to be human along with so many others. If he could just figure out where he had gone wrong, he could save so many lives.

If he marked all of his failed attempts that would be deadly to vampires, vampire hunters would be out of work. He smirked at the thought. That would be a strange twist of fate.

After several deep breaths, he started cleaning up his lab, getting rid of the poison he had accidentally created and lowering the fire on the other ones he was still working on. It did not take long before he turned and made his way up the worn stone stairs that took him from his laboratory to the manor proper. He and Eleonor had lucked out with the property, and he loved the home they had made together.

They had never mentioned it before, but Max knew if things had been different, they would have filled the halls with the sound of children's footsteps. Unfortunately, that was not in the cards for vampires. Just another thing that had been stolen from them. He tried not to dwell on these types of thoughts. He had Eleonor, and that was enough for him. She was the love of his life, both the living and the dead parts.

He wandered from room to room until he found Eleonor on the balcony off their bedroom. She was gazing up at the stars, a worry line present between her eyebrows. Coming up from behind, he wrapped his arms around her, and she turned to give him a kiss.

It was chaste, but Max could still taste her last meal on her lips. Love for her crashed over him and he wished he could erase the sadness in her eyes and the worry on her face. When Eleonor was happy, she lit up the entire room and her laughter was contagious. But sometimes she became despondent, and Max would do everything in his power to make her feel better. The weight of what they were weighed on her more than it did on him.

Before he could ask her what was wrong, she told him. "The joy from feeding is gone. In the beginning, the rush I felt when the blood first touched my tongue was indescribable but now… now I hate it. I barely made it through my meal tonight without throwing up. It was absolutely horrible." She shuddered in his arms.

"You deserve nourishment, my love," Max whispered, running his thumb between her brows to ease the crease. "You know we need to eat so we don't go feral. You know not eating puts everyone in danger, and that's the last thing we want. You can't start throwing up your meals, Eleonor. That's just a waste."

Eleonor shook her head. Max did not know if it was in acknowledgment or denial of what he had said. "Every time I drink from someone, every time I kill someone, all I can think of is my parents being killed in the same manner. Am I no better than the monster that killed them? The monster that stole my childhood from me and turned me into one of them? Is that all I've become?"

"That's why we only feed on criminals if we can, Eleonor," Max pointed out, trying to comfort her. They had developed a system over the years where their victims were the less desirables of society. Killing and drinking from a murderer gave back to society in a way. At least, that was what they liked to think.

She nodded gravely. "Tonight, I watched my victim nearly beat a man to death for an imagined offense. I almost wasn't able to stop him before he killed the other man. Even so, the poor man might be crippled for the rest of his life."

"That seems like just the type of man you should feed from. Did something happen?" Max didn't know where she was going with this, but he knew her well enough to recognize she had a point.

"I thought he was a perfect meal," Eleonor whispered. "And then I bit him, and I watched him tickle his son as they rolled around on the floor together. He loved his son very much. His son was the light of his life, and I stripped that from him. Now a son will grow up without a father."

Max hugged her tighter, at a loss for any words of comfort. He wanted to point out that a man who nearly beat someone to death probably was not the best father, but he also had not seen what Eleonor had in the man's memories. Maybe he had been a great father but a bad man.

"No matter what we do, we are monsters. We can try not to be, but at the end of the day, we are." She paused. "Do you believe in hell, Max?"

Max shifted, uncomfortable with the direction the conversation had gone. Instead of giving her a flippant response, he thought about her question. "I would like to believe there is some divine punishment for those that do wrong, so yes, I guess I do."

Eleonor nodded. "I do, too. The only problem is I feel like I'm the one down here making judgments I shouldn't. I'm not qualified to decide someone's fate. I don't even have a soul. How can a soulless being judge another's soul? How do I know that I'm feeding on the right people, Max? What if I'm making mistakes? I have to be, at least some of the time."

Max shook his head. "Eleonor, no one is asking you to judge anybody. You have to feed. You must feed. Starving yourself isn't an option unless you want to go mad with hunger. We are doing the best we can, and that's all anyone can ask of us. Hell, I think we're doing a lot better than other vampires. We're trying, and that's what counts. We're only monsters if we allow ourselves to be, and I'd like to think we won't ever get to that point."

Eleonor gave a small nod that Max almost missed.

"I love you, whether you're a monster or not," Max said before leaning down and kissing her forehead. "I will never give up on you, my love. There are better days ahead. We must persevere. Hope dies last."

She leaned into him, collecting whatever comfort she could and curling her small, cold fingers in the back of his shirt. Max didn't mention the cure he was working on. It was for her. Someday, they would watch the sun rise together. But until it was perfect, he wanted to protect her from disappointment. The weight of their burden was heavy enough for her to carry right now. Holding his beloved tight, he promised her silently that he would find the cure.

For her.

For their future.

CHAPTER TWENTY-ONE

Ellie still felt the cool breeze of that starry night at the manor on her cheeks when she withdrew from the memory. Her teeth were still buried deep in Julian's neck, and he lay motionless beneath her. Her muscles felt frozen and rigid—like they didn't belong or answer to her. His blood ran sweet and constant like a river over her tongue and down her throat. It warmed her belly, and in her brief paralysis, she marveled at how intact Max's memory had been.

She remembered his laboratory in the basement with all its vials, trinkets, open flames, and messy cabinets. She'd wandered through it on occasion, but she never thought to look into what he was researching. His works were his private musings, and she only investigated the subjects he was willing to share.

He had never once mentioned a word of a cure to her before.

Cure.

Was there such a thing? How close had Max come to returning them to their human forms? Would doing so bring their souls back?

Hope dies last.

His words rang in her ears, and they were what jolted her

out of her reverie. Her fangs slid back into her gums. Julian shuddered beneath her, coming back to his own. She stroked his face and called out to him, beckoning him to come back to her and out of the memory.

"Are you okay?" she asked, her voice husky. She kept her face pressed to his chest, listening to his heartbeat, hesitant to look at him after she had literally just drank from him like he was her last meal. There were certain intimacies one expected from your lover, and others crossed a line. She did not know how Julian felt about her drinking his blood and entering his mind.

Julian pulled back slightly to look down at her, forcing her to look at him, and nodded. "I'm okay. I think. Just a little... cold." He paused and stroked her back, letting his fingers trail through her hair. "Did you see what I saw?" His voice seemed normal, as if they were simply discussing the weather as opposed to his deepest memories. His grasp on the situation impressed her.

"Yes." A private moment had been presented, and she was not sure how Julian felt about having it be shared without his consent. Despite her love for Max, there were still things locked inside her head she would prefer he not see. If he asked about her deepest shames, she would share with him, but she would never volunteer the information unless he asked. Some things were too bad for the open air, and she was sure Julian would understand if she brought this to his attention.

He nodded again, his gaze somewhere over her head. Was he replaying the flashes of memories? Was he disgusted? Ashamed? Curious? Jealous of the moment she'd shared with Max on that balcony?

Surely not, she thought, dismissing it.

"This... cure..." She hesitated, trying to find the words for what she wanted to ask. Her brain was going a million miles a minute. When he looked at her, his gaze still far away, she continued. "Were you really trying to find a cure for us?" She knew it was true; she had seen the memory as well. But she wanted confirmation that he had been trying to save them back then.

This human version of Max was still her soulmate, but Julian was more open than Max had ever been. He wore his heart on his sleeve, and Ellie could only guess this was because he had lived a softer life than Max had. He had never spoken at length about his time before becoming a vampire, or the immediate aftermath, but from what Ellie had been able to pull from him, he had struggled through life. It had not been kind to him.

Despite the trauma that Ellie had experienced, she had to admit that her childhood was lost to her, but the time with her adoptive father had been, for lack of a better word, nice. She had been the Coven leader's daughter and had received the respect due to such a position. More or less, she had led a good life. Max had never said he envied her experiences, but he had been short whenever she asked him for details.

"I guess so. It seems like something I would do." He frowned slightly. "I remember having this burning sense of urgency. It felt like time was running out, and I was desperate to complete it before... before..." He trailed off, a frown on his face.

"Before what?" she asked.

Julian shook his head, his frown still in place. "I don't know. I can't remember anything that would put a time limit on my experiments. We were both vampires—it wasn't like we were going to die of old age. We had the time."

"You always did seem a bit on edge when I asked about your projects," Ellie remembered, her own small frown present. "Sometimes I had to drag you away from your work."

Julian took his thumb and smoothed out the crease between her eyebrows. "I think I was close, too. Or at least I believed I was close, despite what that memory said. I think I'd progressed past that point. After seeing that memory and adding in all the other snippets that have returned, I can almost promise that the cure was created. I just don't know why we didn't take it." His voice softened as if he were speaking to himself, not to her. "I have no doubt it worked. I half remember that, at least. But I wonder..."

"Wonder what?"

Julian's arms tightened around her. "I wonder if the cure had any part to play in us being taken by the hunters."

She pushed herself up with her hands upon his chest. "But how would they know?"

"That's a good question, and the part I don't get. It's the only thing that would make sense that could have set someone off. But I still don't understand why a cure for vampirism would have upset anyone. Shouldn't everyone be happy, both vampires and hunters alike? If there was a cure, then vampires wouldn't need to feed off humans, and humans wouldn't need to hunt them down. It would solve all problems, wouldn't it?"

Ellie tried to keep the excitement bubbling up in her under control. Just because Max had been working on a cure did not mean there was a cure. "I've spent hundreds of years lamenting over the weeks leading up to our betrayal and I've never been able to come up with a reason for it. The only people we could ask would be the Coven, and I don't think it would be the best idea for either of us to approach them. I've spent centuries avoiding them, and I'm sure they think I'm dead by now. Lone vampires usually only last a century or two on their own. The solitude drives them mad." She paused and added, "Do you remember anything else about it? The cure, I mean."

Julian sighed and shook his head. "No, I don't. I remember some things that didn't work, even though I had expected them to, but overall, it's a gray spot in my memory. I remember writing everything down in my journal in the same code you brought me, but I don't remember where I put the journal or any specifics about what it contained. For all we know, it went up in flames with the rest of the manor. And before you ask, the notes you gave me aren't about a cure. That recipe was just something I was fiddling with, and it didn't work, so it's just as well, really."

Ellie refused to give up. "Do you remember anything about *making* the cure?"

Tilting his head, he said, "I remember being surprised that making a cure was just like playing around with the alchemy I usually worked with. I thought it was odd that something so important—life-changing, even—was as simple as it was. That one part of this and one part of that had the ability to make our hearts beat again. Whatever the final recipe was. I know the final ingredient was one so common I had initially disregarded it as useless. Whatever it was ended up being the key to making the whole cure work and I felt silly for not trying it sooner. But beyond these general feelings and memories, I have nothing. I do think, with enough time and the right environment, I might be able to recreate it. It would take a lot of work, though, since I'm basically starting from square one again."

For just a moment, Ellie allowed herself to imagine a life—a human life—with Julian. The thought was all-consuming, and she could see a house and kids and something as simple as the carpool line for school as a possibility. They had never talked about kids, but Ellie knew if they had been able to, both she and Max would have wanted some. At least two, maybe three. She had been a bit lonely as a child, as she was always the youngest vampire present, and she didn't want her own kids to feel that way.

Reality settled back in with an uncomfortable snap, and she realized that whatever this cure was, it was as far away now as it had ever been. Julian would have to remember the recipe, and who knew if all the ingredients were things they could get here in New York. He had been working with things that had been present in the 1500s in Europe, and although New York had a lot to offer, she doubted they would be able to find everything here.

"I can't believe how brilliant you are." She glanced at the clock sitting on the desk. There were several hours before dawn, plenty of time for them to work out what their future would hold. And now she didn't have to flee into the dark hours of the morning to be back in her dingy basement suite before dawn. She swallowed her nerves before asking, "What does this mean for us?"

Julian's eyebrows rose. "What do you mean? Now that I've found you again, you aren't leaving. You can't. I can't. Honestly, if you tried, I'd follow you shamelessly."

Ellie let herself laugh. "I'm not going anywhere, Julian. Not now that I know everything and you remember me. But we need to be realistic. You're human, and I'm a vampire. Our lifespans are vastly different." The words were sour in her mouth, and she had to practically spit them out, but she had to make sure Julian understood what he was signing up for by being with her. Things did not just magically work out because he got his memories back.

It wasn't that simple.

Julian hesitated for only a second, but it was long enough for Ellie to notice. "If I need to become a vampire so we can be together, that's all right. We can go wherever we need to go. As long as I have you, everything else is negotiable."

There was no reason for Ellie to doubt his words, but deep down, she knew he would regret turning into a vampire again. Max had been clear that his dearest wish was to be human again, which was what probably inspired him to work on the cure in the first place. "Is that what you want? To be a vampire?"

"No," he answered honestly. "It's not. I remember being Max, but I'm still Julian, too. I don't want to be a killer again."

His words stung. *Killer.* He only spoke the truth—she was a killer. She wished she was the type of person who remembered each and every kill, but she was not. In truth, all her victims had blended together in her mind until they were a blob, their individualities lost to time.

"I would never ask that of you."

Julian nodded and he looked a bit relieved. "I have an idea, if you're open to it."

"Tell me."

"What if we go back to Europe?" He shifted, eagerness lighting up his eyes. "I don't think we will find anything left of the old manor, but it's worth a shot. Maybe going back there will jog my memory and I'll remember the cure."

"But you're in school," Ellie pointed out. "You have a life here. You have—"

"I can take a sabbatical. I can always come back and finish, but I feel like this is more important." He took her by the arms. "Ellie, you're my life now, as you were before."

She licked her lips as that all-too-familiar flood of hope washed over her. Max had always made her feel this way. "Are you sure?"

"Yes. Let's go home."

CHAPTER TWENTY-TWO

Ellie woke just as the sun sank behind Spain's horizon. Turning to look over at Julian, she found he was still asleep. Overall, he had adjusted well to a nocturnal schedule. He hadn't had much of an option, really. Scheduling travel around avoiding sunlight stretched the already inconvenient chore into a maddening one. He maintained patience the whole time but frayed a bit at the edges when their flight was delayed and pressed right up against sunrise when they were due to leave the airport. They'd had to check into the airport hotel, and Ellie hid in the windowless bathroom while he closed the curtains and made sure the room was safe for her.

Since then, they had moved to safer areas to travel. Today, they slept at a quaint inn in a small Spanish town surrounded by rolling hills and farmlands. Soon, they would reach the manor.

After slipping out of bed slowly so as not to wake him, Ellie padded out onto the balcony attached to their room.

Leaning against the rail, she gazed out at the horizon. Sunlight still stained the skyline, but it posed no threat to her. If anything, it just made her a bit sleepy. This was the most sunlight she had seen in years. Most days, she tried not to think of all that she had missed by being a vampire, but there were moments like now that she wondered what she had lost over the years.

A heavy pressure sat on her chest at being back here. She had not been in Northern Spain for centuries. When she had fled, she had never looked back, choosing to forget both where she had come from and the Coven.

With a critical eye, she gazed down at the town center laid out below her. Once, a bonfire had been erected here and lit, right below where she now stood. She would have been able to feel its heat from here. Max had been thrown unceremoniously onto it, his body turning to ash before her eyes.

She had burned this town to ash a thousand times over in her nightmares.

Everything was different now, but the moment they had stepped into town, she had known where they were. She didn't know if Julian was aware of the significance of the town, and she hesitated to inform him. If he didn't feel the heaviness pressing on his chest the way Ellie did, all the better. She could remember for the both of them.

There were still people mulling around the town center, and if she let her mind run wild, she could picture how the town had once looked.

Before the night of their attack, she had come into town only a handful of times. When hunting, she would stick to the outer limits, never going into the town proper. Even though her time had been limited, she still recalled the place in detail. It was amazing what the mind held on to.

There was a shifting sound from the bed, and Ellie didn't need to turn to know Julian was rising. With soft footsteps, he headed toward her. She relaxed into him as he wrapped his arms around her.

"It's beautiful, isn't it?" Julian whispered, gazing down at the town.

Ellie made a noncommittal grunt. "The sky is. The rest of it?" She grunted again.

Julian's soft laugh rumbled through her. "They're long dead, you know. Not the Coven, but those from this town who lit the pyre."

Who killed you, she thought.

"We best get going. We still need supplies," she said.

Julian released her and headed back inside to change.

Just because the sun had set did not mean the stores had closed yet, and they needed supplies. Or, more accurately, Julian needed supplies. Ellie was much heartier than him and really didn't need anything. She had slept in caves many times throughout her life and doing so again would cause no issue.

Julian would laugh at the comparison, but Ellie felt like he was a delicate flower left in her protection. Practically everything could harm him or make him sick, and she felt it was her job to keep him safe. After all, she had fangs, impressive strength, and immortality.

Once ready, they locked the door and set out.

"Where to first?" Ellie asked, slipping her hand into Julian's.

"Let's get the camping stuff first, pack it in the rental car, and then go back for the food. We won't be able to carry everything in one go. We don't have enough arms."

Ellie nodded and pulled him in the direction of the camping store they had passed on their way into town. She could have carried it all, but it would draw unwanted attention.

When they entered the shop, they were greeted by a quick-speaking Spanish salesman. Ellie informed the man what they were looking for in perfect Spanish.

They made quick work in the store, getting everything Julian might need to sleep outside, if not comfortably, at least safely. Although they knew where they were going, the conditions were still unknown.

The helpful salesman asked several times where they were

going, but Ellie brushed him off with a vague answer each time before finally telling him they were going to be traveling around and wanted to be prepared for anything. This seemed to satisfy him as he heaped more onto their pile 'just in case.'

Ellie didn't argue. She really did not have a clue what Julian needed, but walking hand in hand through the town, she felt almost like they were a normal couple getting ready for a normal camping trip. She would give anything to keep this feeling just a little bit longer.

After they had paid and carried the six bags and two backpacks to the car, they circled back around and went to the grocery store.

Most of the items, although in Spanish, were easily identified by Julian. He needed little translations from her this time. Now that Julian remembered what she was, she didn't need to continue eating and waste their food. *His* food.

Once they had paid for their basket full of Julian's food, they packed the car before checking out of their room.

The roads were well lit, but once they got past the edge of town, the roads were swallowed up by darkness. Ellie drove, having more of an idea of where they were going than Julian, along with better night vision. The headlights illuminated bends before they appeared out of nowhere, and every now and then blazed upon a pair of silvery eyes in the dark. Critters and animals of the night. The manor they had shared had been an hour outside of town limits by horse, but with a car, the trip went much faster.

Ellie was surprised to find many of the roads had not changed beyond being paved. When they were about a mile outside of where the manor had once stood, she parked the car and they climbed out. It took a while for them to sort through everything they had bought and pack away only what they needed for the night.

After centuries, Ellie had no idea if anything of the manor

still stood, but she knew where it had been. Vampires did not forget. A memory may lay dormant for centuries in their mind, but it was never really gone.

"Do you know where we're going?" Julian asked as he stumbled over a tree root. They had flashlights out for Julian's benefit, but the light only went so far.

"Kind of," Ellie admitted. "I have a general idea."

"At least you can see," he grumbled, tripping again.

"Do I need to carry you?"

"Very funny. I'm not entirely helpless." After a pause, Julian added, "How much longer do you think it'll be?"

"Not far. I think."

"If we do find the manor, what are we going to do with the car?"

"I figured after we unloaded everything, I could take it back to town and run back."

Julian snorted. "Ellie, we are miles from town. It'll take you forever to get back." She could hear the frown in his voice.

"No, it would take *you* forever to get back."

"Oh. Good point."

Of their own accord, Ellie's steps slowed. Julian almost ran into her before he managed to stop himself.

"It's different, but I recognize the area. We're close." Excitement bubbled up in Ellie as she made her way forward. Julian scrambled behind her, trying to catch up.

The cold stone walls appeared out of nowhere. They both froze, staring at the remains of what once had been their home.

The moonlight lit up the space enough that they could see that the second story was completely gone, either from the fire or time, she did not know. There were still parts of the first floor standing, although it was marked by age and the fire that had consumed it.

Ellie walked forward to press her hand on the cold stone. It was real. They were back where they belonged, even though everything had changed.

Home.

Julian stepped past her and into what was left of their manor. Where floorboards once lay, nothing but dirt remained. His face was stoic, and she wondered if he remembered all the good years they shared here. More than a lifetime's worth.

They passed through what once had been their unused formal dining room and past what was left of the stairs leading to the second floor. There were only three stone steps still standing going up to nowhere. Ellie thought they were very much like her life these past three hundred years. A broken journey to nowhere.

Ellie glanced at Julian and found him searching the ground, clearly looking for something as they passed into the kitchen. Before she could ask him what he was looking for, he gasped and fell to his knees.

"What are you doing?" she asked.

She was answered when he pulled open the trapdoor that had been covered with debris.

"Is that..." She trailed off, staring at the opening.

"My lab." He flashed her a bright smile. "It is."

They peered down into the darkness below. Taking her flashlight, Ellie shined the light down illuminating the stone steps so Julian's eyes could see into the depths.

"I'll go first," she said. When Julian cocked an eyebrow, she rolled her eyes. "There's no need to protect your masculine sensibilities, Julian. If something goes wrong, you and I both know I'm better equipped to handle it."

Julian scooted back, allowing Ellie to step down. "Yes, ma'am."

As she descended, she scanned the lab, looking for any threats. She let her senses fan out ahead of her, searching for an unwelcome presence. She couldn't find any. In fact, besides being dusty from time, everything looked to be the same as it had before the fire. There was no evidence the fire had ever reached this part of the manor.

"Is it safe?" Julian called down.

"Yes, but watch your step. The stairs are steep."

Julian followed her down and paused when he reached the bottom. "Wow."

"I know."

"I think we found where we're going to camp out today."

She nodded. "We better unload the car before the sun rises."

CHAPTER TWENTY-THREE

After they unloaded the car and trekked back to the manor, it was nearly dawn. Since they were going to be sleeping in the lab and were technically inside, they didn't bother with setting up the tent they had bought. Honestly, it was a relief. Ellie may have slept in caves before, but she would prefer to be inside out of the elements while she slept away the day.

They rolled out the mats and sleeping bags they had bought next to one another on the stone floor. They were more for Julian's benefit than her own.

Ellie glanced around once more, taking in the lab. They had placed a few mini lanterns out, saving the candles they had bought for later use. It was a weird combination—the ancient beakers sitting next to the very modern lights. For the first time, Ellie wondered what had happened to the concoctions Max had been working on when they had fled. Was one of the cauldrons filled with the dust of the cure?

It reminded Ellie of how much time had passed. Even for a vampire, three centuries was a long time, and yet somehow, she was back at the manor with the love of her life. She prayed the cyclical nature of time would stop here. She would not survive losing Max again. It would kill her. She was only so strong, and she knew she would never be able to recover if something happened to him.

This time around it would be different. It had to be—fate was not that cruel. At the very least, she hoped it was not.

"You really don't mind sleeping during the day?" she asked, snuggling down in her sleeping bag. Her body did not warm the plush lining. It remained as cold as the ground she lay upon.

"Nah. I've always been a night owl. To be honest, not much has changed. I always struggled waking up in the morning no matter what time I went to sleep." He propped himself up on one elbow and turned to her. "Besides, why would I want to miss out on my time with you and sleep the night away?"

"I worry I cost you too much," she whispered.

Julian shook his head, reached out, and stroked her chin with the back of his hand. "No, my love. You have given me everything and cost me nothing."

They lay in silence for several minutes, and she was just starting to doze when Julian spoke.

"Eleonor?" Julian asked. She heard the huskiness in his voice, and her body reacted immediately. Despite their odd environment, he wanted her. How many times had she and Max made love in this very manor over the years they had lived there?

"Yes?"

"Can you come here for a moment?"

Ellie rolled out of her sleeping bag and turned to face Julian. As soon as she was next to him, he reached out and cupped her cheek, drawing her face near enough to capture her lips with his own. Ellie sighed in pleasure, closing her eyes and focusing on the sensation of his lips on hers.

So warm. So soft. So human.

The kiss was softer than Ellie had expected, more of a

question than a statement. She opened her mouth in invitation, and Julian took it, deepening the kiss. He took his time, making sure every inch of her was explored.

He ran his hand down her side until he cupped her ass and pulled her flush against him.

Despite his slow perusal of her mouth, Julian's body gave her other signals that he was growing impatient for more. She could hear his pulse hastening—a steady, rhythmic, racing drumbeat. It was music to her ears. His blood coursed through his veins in great whooshes, and she felt his length grow hard against her under the sleeping bag.

Playfully, she reached inside the depths of his significantly warm sleeping bag and rubbed him over his pants.

She nipped at his lips and flicked his fly open. "Remove them."

Julian chuckled and struggled to undress within the confines of his sleeping bag. His knees strained against the material as he pulled the pants down. She hastened to remove her clothes, having a much easier time with it, and resisted the urge to tear through his sleeping bag entirely to get to him.

He needed it for warmth later.

She marveled at the way Julian's muscles moved as he reached for her, drawing her near to capture her lips again. When their skin touched each other, both of them shuddered at the sensation. Fire and ice.

This time, there was an urgency to the action, as if Julian was scared she might slip away if he didn't hold her tight enough. She matched his urgency and sank into the kiss. Never in her hundreds of years of dreaming did she ever imagine she would be back in this place with her love.

His cock lay against her thigh, and she reached between them and gently grasped it. The soft skin moved effortlessly against the hard shaft as she gave him an experimental pump.

"Ellie," Julian gasped, pulling back slightly. "If you don't stop,

I'm not going to last very long, and I want to make it last for both of us."

She released him with a pout.

Julian dipped his hand between her legs. "You're so wet."

She hummed in response, letting her legs fall open for better access. The dirt floor bit into her shoulder blades and spine. He slipped first one, then two fingers into her while simultaneously bending his head to capture her pebbled nipple in his mouth. Biting down gently, he increased the pace of his hand.

Ellie squirmed, her need for him increasing with each movement. "Julian," she said. "Please."

It was all the encouragement he needed. He rolled smoothly to his knees and placed himself between her thighs. Dropping his hips, he ran himself across her, teasing her until she lifted her ass from the dirt, daring him to take her.

He teased her, pushing only the tip of his cock in.

"Julian," she gasped.

Instead of responding, he thrust forward, entering her all the way. Ellie moaned as he started pumping into her at a steady rhythm, her senses in overdrive.

Each stroke was measured, and Ellie raised her hips, altering the angle so Julian hit just the right spot.

"Bite me," he whispered roughly in her ear.

Ellie didn't have to be told twice. Sex and blood went together like wine and cheese. Ellie reached for him and drew him down to her. As he thrust deep inside her, she sank her fangs into his neck. Flesh and tendon gave way so easily. She moaned against his throat as blood filled her mouth. She let it build until it was the perfect mouthful, and her eyes rolled back as she swallowed. Cautiously, she braced herself for whatever memory was to flash before her eyes while Julian, hovering over her, still pressed deep inside of her. His breath fluttered deliciously. The muscles in his arms strained. He let out a low growl of pleasure, and she drank more greedily.

The memory flashed behind her closed eyelids. It was one she had relived a thousand times over.

"Are you sure you want to do this?" Max asked, panting.

In the memory, Ellie found herself looking down at her own naked body beneath Max. She saw his hands planted on either side of her, pale skin and flexing tendons oh so familiar to her. She squirmed beneath him. His appreciative eyes roamed her features, searching for any sign of hesitation. There were none.

"For goodness sake, Max, will you please stop talking? I know what we're doing, and I want this just as much as you do."

Through Max's eyes, she saw him reach out and squeeze her hip. The memory was so real she thought she should have felt her own flesh give way beneath his hand, but she couldn't. All she could feel was Julian's blood warming her belly and his cock sliding in and out of her.

"I'm trying to make this good for you," Max said, as his hand fell between her thighs.

Ellie watched her old self bite her bottom lip. "*Take me.*"

"Yes, ma'am." Max chuckled, pushing her legs apart farther so he could slip between them. Positioning himself at her entrance he slowly entered her.

Ellie remembered his hesitancy as she watched it all unfold in her mind's eye. He hadn't wanted to hurt her, he'd told her after. He'd been a fool, really. He couldn't hurt her.

As Max set the rhythm in the memory, Ellie realized Julian was matching it in real time. She didn't know if it was intentional, but the combination of the two sensations was hurtling her toward the edge of bliss faster than she would have thought possible.

"Ellie," Julian moaned, just as Max whispered, "*Eleonor.*" With each thrust, she was brought close to her own orgasm until she spiraled out of control. Julian followed suit, filling her with cum as Max climaxed. Ellie pulled back from his neck, scared if she didn't, she might take too much blood from him.

The double experience was enough to leave them both gasping. Julian collapsed onto her. His bare chest swelled with every breath, and she relished the warmth of him on top of her. She gently stroked his back as they came back to their senses.

"Wow," Julian said.

She hummed in agreement, still lost somewhere between bliss and time.

"I love you," Julian whispered.

"I love you, too."

CHAPTER TWENTY-FOUR

It was odd being back at the manor, not because they had been gone for so long but because so little of it was left standing. Despite its condition, Ellie felt more at home than she had in centuries, although she didn't know if that was from being back or being with Julian. After some thought, she decided it was probably a combination of both.

After their first day there, Ellie did a thorough inspection of the manor and found some of the rooms were mostly intact. She needed to figure out how to put a new roof up in some spots because the stones that had once been there had collapsed in, but the overall structure was sturdy. It was incredible to see how the place had survived not only time, but also the fire that had scorched through it.

It felt good to keep her hands busy as she started on the necessary repairs. She had always been handy, and now she had the opportunity to use her skills. Julian had offered to help, but she had brushed him off knowing he had more important things to do. Besides, she could move at an infinitely faster rate, and she didn't want to hurt his feelings by telling him he'd just get in the way.

Julian spent his days in the lab working obscene hours on the cure. Ellie tried her best to give him space and not distract him. He was focused on finding the cure again no matter the cost it took on his physical well-being. He was obsessed, determined to find the combination that would save Ellie. Most days, she had to remind him to eat and drink water. He was so focused that he forgot.

"I need a favor," Julian announced, popping his head up from the lab trap door.

"What is it?" She arched an eyebrow as she lowered an armful of cut wood to the dirt floor. She intended to use it for a new floor, or perhaps to start a fire if the evenings continued to grow colder. Julian would need warmth. Sleeping with her every night literally cost him his own body heat.

He gave her a bright smile. "I may need you to commit a crime."

Ellie folded her arms, waiting for him to continue. Julian and Max had both been rule followers, and she wondered what he needed so badly.

"I need a UV lamp."

"And where am I supposed to find one of those?" she asked.

"Just find a tanning salon and break in." He said it so causally Ellie didn't immediately process what he was saying. He might as well have been talking about the weather, which had been especially pleasant lately.

"A tanning salon? In the Spanish countryside?"

He nodded. "Ordering one online would be too difficult. Where would they even deliver it to? And let's not even talk about the price for the one I would need. It'll be easier for you to just steal one for me."

"You want me to go commit several crimes, including breaking and entering and theft. Am I getting this straight?"

He nodded as if this was the most normal thing he could ask of her. "Well, yes. And don't get caught. That would create way too many issues. I don't speak Spanish well enough to bail you out of jail."

Ellie rolled her eyes. "Thanks for looking out for me."

"I love you." He beamed at her. They both knew she would do as he asked. She had already gone collecting local herbs for him several times. This assignment was not much different. At least, she told herself it was not. After centuries of living on the edge of what was right and what was wrong, her morals might be a little warped. Besides, tanning salons had insurance, right?

Ellie spent several hours browsing the internet, trying to find the best tanning salon to break into. As she scrolled, she marveled at how much easier things were now. They had bought a solar generator at the camping store and had been keeping their cell phones charged in case of an emergency. It had been pricey, but it was not that large and it charged enough during the day that they could use it all night.

There was a salon relatively close by—and by close by, she meant forty-seven miles—but it was a small business, and she knew they would struggle to replace the expensive light. Not only that, she didn't want to be too close to the manor. The last thing she wanted to do was commit a string of robberies and have them be traced back to them.

Instead, she chose a city a little farther away that had a chain of shops. Replacing a UV lamp would be much easier for them, and that dampened some of the guilt she felt at the crime.

The next night, Ellie kissed Julian goodnight and headed toward town. Despite what Julian thought, it really wasn't that far of a journey for her. She jogged, and with her superhuman speed, she was there in less than an hour, looking none the worse for her exercise. Julian had pressed her to rent a car, but she didn't need the extra risk. Cars had license plates, and rental places required names and ID, and the last thing they needed was for local authorities to connect a car rental to a breaking and entering and robbery.

No, she would do this the old-fashioned way. On foot.

Tonight, it really felt like she was back in time several hundred years—until she happened upon her targeted salon with a neon sun over the front door that buzzed obnoxiously as she avoided passing under its yellow glow. She had to stay out of sight.

BREAKING into the tanning salon was much easier than she had anticipated. She forced open the back door of the shop, likely the entrance used to take out the garbage or accept deliveries of products like tanning oils, sunscreens, and whatever other chemical-induced nonsense humans put on their skin before they paid good money to punish their delicate skin. She had not bothered with any tools, knowing that she could take any door off with her bare hands, given the right motivation.

She slunk into the salon, using her keen night vision to detect obstacles and skirt them. She kept her head down, low to the ground, and ducked into the first private tanning room she reached. A tanning bed lay against one wall, and when she lifted the lid, she realized she was ill-equipped to remove the light. She considered it for a passing moment, wondering if she should give it a try before deciding to try the stockroom instead. A place like this must have had backup lights in case one of the tubes in the bed went out.

Her hunch paid off. In a rather messy storage room, she found multiple UV lights and took three for herself, leaving them plenty. Hell, they might not notice any were gone until they did inventory—if a place with such messy storage did inventory at all. She crept out the back door into the unlit lane behind the shop, closed the door behind her, and let it rest there. She'd broken the handle so it wouldn't lock, but she didn't want to leave the door ajar in case some other unsavory folk like herself got the bright idea to rob them a second time over.

She removed her sweater and used it to tie the tube lighting across her back, somewhat like a satchel. Once they were good and secure, she left town the same way she had come, vanished into the shadows of the countryside, and ran.

It was nearly dawn by the time she got back, and Julian was waiting for her at the place where they had parked the car last time.

He moved toward her as she slowed to a walk. "I was worried you weren't going to make it by sunup," he said, holding up a large sheet he used to cover precious items in his lab.

She smiled. "You brought that for me?"

"Just in case the sun came up."

She eyed the horizon. Pale light illuminated the silhouettes of trees in the distance. "We have time, but we should hurry."

"Is this all that you need?" she asked once they were back in the lab.

Julian nodded, his eyes far away. She knew he was thinking hard about whatever process he needed the lamp for.

"It's a good thing we bought the solar-powered generator at least," she said. "Otherwise, this would be completely useless."

Ellie lay down on their makeshift bed and watched Julian move around the laboratory as if it was his second home. She had some sense it really was. He spent all his time here, and he'd come to the habit of working way past when she'd already gone to sleep.

"Are you really going to be working on this all day?" she asked with a yawn.

He shook his head and then paused. "Well, maybe, I'm not sure. I'm in the middle of something right now and I just want to make sure that it's done correctly."

Ellie picked lint from her blankets.

"Are you going to go on a hunting trip tomorrow?" he asked.

Ellie wanted to say no, but instead, she nodded. "Yeah, it's about time." Although she had been feeding on Julian when they were having sex, she hadn't had a real meal in days and that was dangerous for both of them. The whole point of Julian being human was to *keep* him human, not to make him into a vampire.

ELLIE MADE her way out of town and traveled a few hours away the following night, just after dusk. She was scared that if she fed too close to home, there would be suspicion. She was careful to only pick from big cities and to dispose of the bodies in ways that looked almost natural. She had learned over the years how to draw suspicion away from vampires, not that any modern-day cop would consider the possibility. That was one benefit—the cops nowadays would look for every excuse other than vampires to explain a death.

Being back in her home country also posed the issue of potentially drawing the attention of other vampires. She knew the Coven was still active in the area, and the last thing she wanted to do was draw their attention to her and Julian.

It was best to let the traitors believe she and Max were good and dead.

Despite the known risks, she had to feed.

She prowled the countryside, alone and hungry, and felt like the animal she was. Hunting in the alleys of New York City had let her believe that she belonged amongst the people there, but here, in the wilderness on the outskirts of small Spanish towns, she couldn't deny the monster that she was. Some nights, if not most, she returned to the manor with an empty belly. Julian would ask how it went, and she saw in the drawn lines of his face and the thinness of his smile that he didn't actually want to know the details. All he wanted to know was that she was fed. She would lie and tell him she was full, and she would remain hungry for a few more days before hunting again.

This ritual continued, and she began to worry that if she

didn't feed soon, she would have to deny Julian sex. And it didn't just feel like sex anymore. It had become this wild, exciting, beautiful thing between them. It made her feel closer to Max and Julian all at once. She didn't want to lose that. But if they kept going at such a rate, and she didn't feed, she feared she would drink him dry.

At the end of the day, she knew she could and would succumb to her urges.

Just like a man needed water, she needed blood.

Soon.

Getting home from an unsuccessful hunt a week later, Julian met her outside of the lab. She wondered how long he had been waiting for her.

"What is it?" she asked, thinking that something might be wrong.

Julian beamed at her. "I think I found the cure."

Ellie blinked. All these hours in the lab, the sleepless days and nights, the restless tossing and turning of his insomnia… had it all finally paid off? "Are you serious?"

"I'm pretty sure I did, but I need to test it on your blood first. If you'll let me."

Ellie nodded and followed him down into the lab. He took her hand to prick her finger with a pin, but she unsheathed her fangs and did it herself, licking her own blood from the tip of one sharp tooth. She dropped a few dollops of blood into the vial he held out to her. Taking the concoction that he made, Julian dropped a single drop in with the blood.

Where her blood had been thick and sluggish, it suddenly turned bright red and thinned out. They both stared at it as if it was growing a second head.

"Do you see what I see?" she asked.

"I do."

"What does it mean?"

Julian's smile faltered a bit. "It means we have to test it on a vampire."

Ellie's excitement dimmed slightly. "Oh."

How can we continue to lay low while simultaneously plucking a vampire from the region and turning them human?

"This is going to be complicated, Julian."

He nodded. "Then we'd better make a plan."

CHAPTER TWENTY-FIVE

Now that they knew what the next part of the plan was, Ellie threw herself into trying to find a vampire they could test the cure on. Knowing that the cure was still in the test stages, she wanted to find a test subject that deserved whatever may happen. She knew there were vampires out there that may not be classified as good but were definitely not bad, and she didn't want to punish them. She wanted to find someone who would not be missed.

Someone foul.

With Julian's help, she scoured the internet, searching for any string of unsolved murders in the surrounding area. She wanted something close enough that she could be there and back in one night but not in the town they bordered. After a bit of research, they found a series of bodies that had been discovered an hour away, all with the same markings, although the police would not explain what those markings were to the media. A rumor had gotten out, though, that the victims had been drained of blood. It was exactly what they had been searching for.

"Are you sure that this is a vampire thing?" Julian asked for the third time. He wore a slight frown, and she knew if there had been any other alternative, he would have jumped at it.

"Yes, of course," Ellie said, scrolling through the news article. "All the signs are there. All we need to do is go to the town and find the guy. He drained a teenager, Julian. A single mother. A janitor. These are all normal people who deserve to still be here. This is our vamp."

"I want to come with you," Julian said somewhat defiantly.

"Absolutely not."

"Why not?"

Why do you even need to ask?

"You know why, Julian. This is a dangerous mission. I'm built for this fight. You are not. You have to stay here so that when I return, we can move forward with phase two. Without you, this thing is dead in the water." She moved to him and took his hand in hers, threading her cold fingers through his warm ones. She squeezed. "I will be careful, I promise."

Secretly, Ellie itched for the fight. She hadn't used any of her training in years, but she used to be an excellent fighter. Despite her small size, she was fast and precise, and that was a deadly combination. She had been known to take Max down despite his size and power advantage. No matter how many times she did it, he was always surprised.

Julian pouted for a moment but didn't argue further. "I hate that I'm a liability to you."

"Don't say that. You're not a liability. You already saved my life just by walking into Thoth's bookstore when you did." She stretched to the tips of her toes to give him a kiss. The crease between his brows eased, and she took this as a sign to continue with the pressing issue of her mission. "I'm hoping this is a young male vampire. They're reckless and much more willing to operate outside of their range of skills. He will underestimate me. Hopefully, he is either newly turned or a loner."

Julian's frown returned, as did the creases in his brow. "And if he's a Coven member?"

"Then we have to hope that I cover my scent well enough, and none of the others come looking for us," she said. "It's one of the risks, Julian. Unless..."

"No," he said firmly.

"I'm willing. You can test it on me. We can—"

"I said no, Ellie," he growled. "I don't know if this is going to work, and if I destroyed you in the name of an experiment?" He shook his head fiercely. "I won't do it. We're supposed to be together. This will not end by corrupting your blood. You're right. We find the killer in the hills and we test it on him. I trust you."

Ellie kissed him again. "We have tonight. I'll track him tomorrow when the sun goes down. I want to feel you."

Julian kissed her back, breathing her in, and gathered her up in his arms. Tonight, all Ellie wanted was to have this moment with him. Everything else could wait.

THE NEXT NIGHT, Ellie took extra time getting ready. She had mainly only packed comfortable items when they had left New York, but she had grabbed a sundress and stuffed it in her bag just in case. She silently thanked her previous self for the foresight. She had imagined it might be used on a date with Julian if they ever got the chance, not to hunt down a vampire.

If this vamp was a male, she might be able to lure him in close with her good looks.

"You look beautiful," Julian said, giving her a lingering look. There was no doubt in her mind that if they had not been on a time crunch, they would have ended up back in bed. "Do you have your tools?"

She patted the bag over her shoulder. "Stake, silver blades, holy water. Check."

"Good luck." As an afterthought, he added, "Don't get hurt, Ellie, I need you."

She nodded. "I'll be fine. I'll be back before dawn. It will be like I never even left."

The murders were only a few towns over, and she was there after only an hour of running at an even pace. The wind felt good against her skin, and her dress fanned out around her as she wove through trees and leapt over branches.

It was Friday night, and downtown was bustling. After careful consideration, she entered the town square with a smooth stride and a bashful tilt of her head. Walking with too much confidence and her chin up might mark her as a harder target than a soft, shy young woman. If she was out hunting for a meal, she would want easy prey and the drunk humans stumbling around would be perfect. Taking into account the assumption that the vampire was probably young and inexperienced, it was more than likely he had had the same thought process.

This was the perfect hunting ground.

She wandered the busy streets, intentionally making herself look every part the aimless tourist. There were tons of people out, but there was not anyone who fit the ethereal beauty of a vampire. The movies had not gotten everything wrong—vampires really were unnaturally attractive. It was both a blessing and a curse sometimes.

The end of the night was nearing when she finally spotted him. If she had a beating heart, it would have skipped.

He came out of one of the clubs that were in the process of closing, a young woman on his arm. She looked too young to be in the club at all, and Ellie's stomach turned over at the thought of what he had planned for her. He walked with his eyes on her throat as the young woman threw her head back and laughed. She was intoxicated, dark-haired, and beautiful. Her skin was bronzed, and Ellie wondered dimly if she spent a lot of time in the tanning beds at the local salon.

The vamp looked like he had stepped out of painting, his features perfectly proportional and strong. Even Ellie had to admit that he was a handsome man, even by vampire standards. His skin was predictably fair, his eyes as black as his hair, limbs long and elegant like a dancer. He moved with distinguished grace, leading the woman through cobblestone streets that continued to narrow and wind until they abandoned the busier parts of town. He had a strategy, that much was clear.

Ellie kept her distance as he led the intoxicated woman down a dark lane flanked by closed-down businesses. Ellie strained her ears and couldn't hear a soul around.

They were alone.

The woman stumbled, and he steadied her with ease, muttering something about her clumsiness that made her giggle. She was oblivious to the danger she was in. A naïve nineteen-year-old, out on the town, about to be bled dry because she was in the wrong place at the wrong time.

Ellie's stomach knotted.

Going about killing the lechers of society was one thing, but killing innocents was another. But taking advantage of the incapacitated was unspeakable; it was on an entirely different level and she felt ill. She had been that woman once—a little girl attacked by the monsters that killed her family. Any guilt she might have felt toward kidnapping the vampire vanished. She would be doing the world a favor if the cure did not work, and he died.

She would feel no pity as he writhed in agony.

When the couple reached the far back corner of the alley shrouded in darkness, Ellie made her move.

Taking the stake from the handbag she carried, she silently stepped forward, keeping to the shadows and darkest corners of the alley.

Neither of them noticed her. The vamp was too focused on the fluttering pulse point on the woman's neck, and she was too focused on his mouth. Ellie could only assume his fangs had extended. The woman gave a coy giggle as he positioned her against the mildewy wall of the alley. The shoulder of her dress slipped down, revealing even more skin. The vamp trailed kisses over it. The woman lifted a leg. She wanted him. He oozed sex appeal. She whispered something to him and began removing the other shoulder of her dress, bearing everything to the creature intent on killing her.

Ellie slunk closer. Her steps were silent. She gripped the stake so hard the wood left imprints on her palm. When she was close enough, she saw his fangs were out. The drunken woman was oblivious. His teeth grazed her throat, and a bead of blood swelled and trickled down. He licked it away, purring like a wild cat.

Ellie leapt from the darkness.

She slammed the stake through his back. Flesh, muscle, and lung gave way. He let out a halted gurgling sound. Ellie gave the stake a firm strike at the end with the heel of her hand, driving it deeper and into his heart. He swayed before tipping over and away from the now terrified woman. He landed hard on his side, black blood spilling out of his chest and into the cracks of the stones.

The young woman staggered backward with a strangled cry. Her eyes flew wildly from Ellie to the man on the ground. "Don't hurt me!"

Ellie took several steps back, giving the woman space. "He was going to hurt you," she said, keeping her voice low and calm, almost melodic. "Look."

The woman looked down, her whole body shaking, and after a moment's inspection, spotted the fangs. Another moment and he would have been attached to her neck, drinking away.

"Are those..." She gasped, unable to finish the sentence. Her voice was slurred with alcohol, and she swayed where she stood.

"Don't worry about it. You're safe now. Forget you ever saw anything." Ellie nodded toward the mouth of the alley. "Go home."

Ellie knew that she should kill the woman. Leaving any witnesses was dangerous for everyone and as scared as the woman was now, Ellie feared she would remember this part of the night. Trauma had a way of sticking with someone, even if they were drunk.

But she couldn't do it. She had not killed an innocent in years, centuries even, and she was not about to start now. The woman was terrified and drunk, and hopefully she would think this was all a dream come morning.

Flicking out her fangs and baring them at the woman, she fought back the guilt when the human jumped back hitting the dirty wall with a thud. "You will never speak of this again. Do you understand?"

The woman nodded several times, too scared to speak.

"And don't leave a club with a guy you don't know," Ellie added. "Especially one who looks like this."

Satisfied, Ellie picked up the vampire into a standing position, resting his head on her shoulder and wrapping her arm around him. To the average eye, it would look like she was helping her drunk friend stumble home. The stake in his back was barely sticking out and was virtually invisible in the night. No one would question them.

Halfway down the alley, the woman called out, "Thank you." Ellie could tell she meant it, too. Even though Ellie had scared her, the woman knew on some level what she had just been saved from.

"You're welcome," Ellie said without turning around.

She carried the incapacitated vamp out of the downtown

core, keeping to the quiet streets. His head lolled and his eyes rolled, but he never managed to come to completely.

That was for the best.

She managed to get him out of town without drawing any attention, and when they were alone and in the cover of the surrounding trees, she draped him over her shoulder like a scarf and held on to him by his belt.

Then she ran like hell to make it back to the manor before dawn.

CHAPTER TWENTY-SIX

Ellie drove her heel down on the trapdoor in the floor of the manor as a way of knocking. The unconscious vamp still lay over her shoulder, and his black blood had dripped all the way down her back and stained her calves and pretty dress as she ran.

Julian's head emerged from the trapdoor first. He blinked up at her in the darkness. "You found him?"

She adjusted the creature on her shoulder. "I did, and he's just as wicked and twisted as I'd hoped."

Julian held the door open the rest of the way. "Come on, bring him down."

Ellie carried the vamp down the stairs. A slab of stone sat in the middle of the lab. Centuries ago, she and Max had carried it down here together. The thing weighed several tons and had taken both of their supernatural efforts to place in his lab. He used it as a table more often than not, but today, it had a more sinister purpose.

They strapped the vamp down, securing every moveable body part except his head with chains doused in holy water and coated in silver. Now was not the time to take risks. Not when they were so close.

Julian eyed the beast nervously as he began fidgeting with his cure, inspecting vials, and gnawing nervously at the inside of his cheek.

Meanwhile, Ellie crouched down so she was eye-level with the vamp and waited.

Soon enough, he would stir.

He would beg.

Perhaps he would even weep.

Good.

"How long do you need?" Ellie called to Julian without taking her eyes off the unconscious vamp.

"Twenty minutes, at most."

The minutes ticked by with agonizing slowness. Ellie grew bored of watching the slumbering vamp and began pacing. She eyed the stake still protruding from his chest and hated how much it reminded her of the night Max died. She knew the exact level of pain the vamp was experiencing. She'd felt it herself, and she had watched her love succumb to that powerlessness and accept his own demise.

Anger coursed through her.

Max had lost everything, and he was one of the good ones. This stain on society had been feeding from good people for who knew how long. If she hadn't shown up, there'd be a bloodless young woman lying in the streets of the small town this very minute, and more than likely a mother to get a terrible phone call or house visit from the police the next morning to inform her that her baby girl was dead.

She hated what he was, and in turn, hated what she was.

This cure *had* to work. She didn't want to be this way anymore. She was tired from not feeding enough, and after all these centuries, she finally felt hope. She could not lose that again. She feared it would destroy her, and now that she had access to the tome that held all the answers to her demise, she knew if worse came to worst, she would end it all.

Perhaps after Julian died of old age.

"Done." Julian lifted a vial of the cure from its holder on one of his workstations and held it up to one of the lamps powered by the generator. He squinted at it and nodded confidently. "This looks the purest so far. It just might work this time, Ellie."

Just then, as she was about to rush to Julian and kiss him, the vamp stirred.

She and Julian both froze and watched as his eyes fluttered open and confusion registered on his handsome face. He blinked up at the stone ceiling before managing to turn his head from side to side. He sniffed at the air, scowled, and sought her out.

"You," he hissed between clenched teeth, fangs bared.

Ellie lifted her chin. "Me."

He strained against his chains. They pulled tight, flexed, and grated against the stone, but did not break. Ellie moved forward and Julian reached out and grabbed her arm. He didn't possess the strength to stop her, but she halted anyway.

"Don't," he warned. "We should just get this over with."

The vamp let out a high-pitched shriek. Julian clamped his hands over his ears and swore.

Ellie rushed the stone slab and struck the vamp across the jaw. "Silence!"

The last thing they needed was for the wrong person—or *thing*—to hear him wailing away like a banshee.

She spun to Julian. "We have to do it now."

Julian came forward, vial in his hands, and the vampire began to squirm.

"What is that? What are you doing? What *is* that?" he cried, thrashing and struggling, eyes flicking wildly from the vial to Julian's handsome face. "Don't. Please. Whatever this is, whatever this is about, I didn't do it. I swear, I didn't do it! I'm new at this," he added, eyes flying to Ellie. "I was bitten two years ago. I'm alone! If there are rules or laws, I didn't know! I didn't break them on purpose. Please. Please. Please!"

Julian's resolve waned. She could feel it in the way his footsteps slowed and his gaze went from her to the vampire, as if looking for her to admit out loud that maybe this wasn't such a good idea after all. But her resolve remained steadfast. She knew what this creature was, and if they let him go, nothing would change. She and Julian would still be trapped in a sort of endless limbo, and they would never know if his experiment was working or not.

"He's already dead." Ellie turned to Julian. "I will do it."

The vampire continued to beg for his life on the table as Julian transferred the contents of the vial into a syringe. Once he'd pushed the air out of it, he handed it to Ellie and told her how to administer it. She didn't mind being the one who had to do it. After all, she was the one who'd gone out and caught the vampire. Without her, none of this would happen anyway, so she was basically the one with blood on her hands.

She hovered over the vampire's arm with the needle.

This could be it. All of Max's work amounted to this moment. He'd never made it far enough all those centuries ago to test his creation on vampires, everything had just been theoretical. She hoped that it worked, especially after all the hours and sleepless nights Julian had poured into it, as she pricked the vampire's vein in his inner elbow and pressed the contents of the syringe into him.

At first, nothing happened.

He stared down at his arm. "What was that? What did you just give me?"

Julian reached out and pulled Ellie into him. He wrapped his arms around her and rested his chin on her head, and she clung to his arms around her front. She wondered how long it would take but didn't have the gall to ask. They waited. Seconds gave way to nearly a minute, and she was beginning to think nothing was going to happen when, all of a sudden, the vampire seized.

Julian tensed behind her.

The vampire's mouth opened wide. His fangs extended and dissolved before their eyes, melting onto his tongue and burning away flesh. No sound came out of him as the same thing happened in his throat. Black blood around the stake in his chest turned bright red—*human* red—and began pouring out of him onto the ground.

Ellie covered her nose and gagged. It smelled awful.

Julian dragged her further from the slab and vampire as blood began pouring out of his eyes and mouth. He shook and seized until all at once he went completely still upon the stone. All the tension against the chains went away.

The putrid smell hung heavy in the air.

Was that it? Was something else supposed to happen?

Julian released her and moved to the experiment. Ellie could hear his heart pounding in his chest, but it was the only heartbeat in the room. The vamp had not returned to his human form. He was either dead, or just a mangled vampire on the slab of stone.

"Julian," she whispered, "don't get too close."

Julian kept his distance but before long turned back to her and told her that the vampire was dead. Not *undead*, but actually dead.

Ellie couldn't understand.

This was supposed to work. They had been so careful and studious, they'd checked every box and made the long journey all the way back to Spain and their manor. If it couldn't work here, it couldn't work anywhere.

She felt dismay seep into her bones. It was a familiar feeling, the same one she'd carried with her before Julian found her.

He begged her not to despair as they began cleaning up, but it was not a plea she could answer. She was so tired. Not in the sense that Julian might have been, where he probably felt it in his body and mind, but tired in her soul. Not that she had one. She couldn't explain it. After they cleaned, she went to lie down and stared up at the ceiling of the lab.

How much longer could she do this?

Julian came and lay down beside her, but he didn't say anything. There was nothing to say. They'd failed. She'd journeyed into town for nothing. Sure, she'd saved the woman who was about to be feasted upon, but even that fact felt hollow.

"We still have time," Julian said, laying a hand on her thigh.

She rolled away from him and tucked her hands under her icy cheek. She should never have come here with him. She should have stayed well enough away and listened to her gut all those weeks ago when she realized that Max's soul was intertwined with Julian's. He would have been better off without her. He could have finished his studies and continued living in his beautiful home in the city he loved so much, and after time healed the heartbreak, he would move on from her and meet someone who could stand in the sunlight with him.

Someone he could marry on a sunny summer afternoon while the flowers were in bloom and the bees buzzed lazily amongst their petals.

Despite her rejection of his touch, Julian turned over with her, gathered her up in his arms, and tucked his chin into the groove of her shoulder. "Hope dies last," he whispered, her voice sounding just like Max's used to. "We can't give up."

CHAPTER TWENTY-SEVEN

Ellie was struggling to hunt and capture vampires. There weren't enough hours in the night for her to do both. Even though her hunger felt like holes burning through her gut, she knew she had to focus her energy on capturing vampires for Julian's experiments. She might have lost hope it would work, but Julian hadn't faltered. He still believed there was a cure out there for her, and his determination was running him ragged. Through bouts of her own hunger, she remained conscious of his needs and made sure he ate and drank water frequently. If she didn't remind him, he would forget for over a day at a time, and his hands would get shaky and he'd start making silly mistakes.

Now was not the time for such errors.

He sat on the dirt floor of his lab eating while Ellie searched the internet. She had tabs on a few suspicious murders in the area that she had a feeling were not victims of the vampire who had died in their captivity a week ago. She kept refreshing the tab to see if another murder joined the list, and when one did, her suspicions were confirmed.

She announced to Julian that night at dusk that she'd found another one, and she was going to go grab it for them.

Julian frowned. "Are you strong enough?"

She pretended she didn't understand his question as she slung her bag over her shoulder. "I won't be long."

"Ellie."

"This one is closer than the last, and I think it's feral." She bent down to retrieve one of the silver blades that slipped out of her bag, and when she straightened, the room spun. She gripped Julian's arm in surprise more than anything. The dizziness passed within seconds, and she gave her head a shake to clear her senses.

"What was that?"

"Nothing."

"That wasn't nothing." Julian turned her around to face him and stared into her eyes. "When did you last feed?"

"I don't know, a day or two ago."

"Why are you lying to me?"

She shoved his hands down. He was always on her case about something these days. "I'm not lying, Julian."

"You haven't fed since before we ran the test. You need blood, Ellie. I can see it in your eyes. You won't make love to me. You'll hardly let me touch you."

It was true.

Sex was off the table. She didn't trust her own self-control. Not feeding enough had made her feel frayed and pulled tight all at once. She was scared that if she were intimate with Julian, she would bite him, and this time she would not be able to stop herself. Just the thought of his sweet blood filling her up made her mouth water.

She licked her lips. "We have more important things to worry about."

He shook his head. "No, we don't. I have more work to do,

and you need to feed. Let this feral vampire have one more night of freedom before you catch him. Feed tonight, hunt tomorrow. Please, Ellie? None of this will work without you. I need you to take care of yourself." He stroked her cheek. "Do it for me?"

Ellie tracked the human to his farm, about thirty miles from the manor. It smelled like manure, sweat, and iron. Old farm equipment hung in the barn where, earlier in the evening, she'd heard him beating his wife. He was cutting wood with an axe he'd just sharpened, his sweat permeating the air. She crept into the barn, staying low, footsteps whispering across the hay-strewn ground.

He never heard her coming.

She leapt out of the darkness from under the loft like a bat, knees tucked, arms splayed wide, and brought him down by his shoulders. He let out a short yell before she sank her teeth into his neck, perched on the balls of her feet on one of his broad shoulders. She rode him to the ground, where he landed heavily. The axe tumbled from his arms, and by the time he gathered his wits, he'd lost too much blood to put up any kind of a fight.

His memories flashed in her mind's eye.

She saw through his eyes as he beat his wife, who begged him to stop. She saw him do atrocious things to other people when he drank too much. He was a violent person with no moral compass, and she drank greedily, letting his blood fill her up and ooze into all her aching places. Julian was right. She had needed to feed.

When she was done, she stepped away from the corpse and licked his blood from her teeth. He wasn't the best meal she'd ever had, but he'd been large, and his blood would hold her over for at least a few days. Hopefully, that was all she and Julian needed.

As she ran back to the manor, she wondered if this was the

last time she would ever have to drink someone's blood. If Julian was successful on his next trial, she might never have to feed like this again. She could indulge in the simplicities humans seemed to love so much, like drinking coffee and eating baked treats. She always suspected that if she were human, she'd be the sort of woman who spent early mornings on café patios, enjoying fresh baked croissants or scones.

Back at the manor, she found Julian working away in his lab, shuffling around like he was in a daze. She announced that she'd fed, and he looked up, not having noticed she came through the trapdoor at all. He managed a small smile before getting back to his work.

She didn't want to distract him, so she went to lie in her bed, where she watched him work for a couple of hours before he began rubbing tiredly at his eyes.

"You need a break," she said.

He resisted. It was like him to want to keep working. He resented the limits of his human body.

She took his hand and dragged him away from his work. He knew he couldn't resist her and let her lead him up out of the trapdoor and up the stairs she'd been working on these past few weeks. Slowly but surely, the manor was beginning to look like the skeleton of its old self. Most of the walls were still missing. The stone fireplace still stood proudly in the middle of the home, and she'd begun framing, but for the most part, it was still but a hollow shell. However, up the stairs and to the right, and through what used to be their bedroom, she had managed to put their balcony together.

Or most of it, anyway.

There were no railings, so she pulled him down to sit with her on the newly floored surface.

"I didn't know you'd finished this," he said.

"It's not done yet." She curled up in his lap, and he crossed his legs around her. "Soon, though. Maybe."

He kissed the top of her head. "Do you feel better?"

She nodded. "Thank you for making me go. I spent such a long time taking care of myself that I'm not used to being told what to do."

He chuckled softly, and the sound rumbled in his chest against her back. "You always were stubborn."

"Me?" She twisted and looked up at him. "You're one to talk."

He tipped his head back and gazed up at the stars. She admired the cut of his jaw and the flutter of his pulse at his throat. So vulnerable and beautiful all at once, and he was all hers. They'd been arguing more these days. Both of them were running out of patience. She knew she was testing him, but she hadn't noticed the strain her lack of feeding and withholding of sex was putting on him.

She could change that now that she'd fed.

She turned around in his arms and wrapped her legs around his waist. Julian gave her a little smile as she stole his attention from the stars.

She draped her hands behind his neck and let her fingers wander up into his hair. "No matter what happens, I will love you forever."

"Forever," he breathed before she silenced him with a needy kiss.

He held her to him, and his hands wandered down to her legs and slipped under the skirts of her dress. His touch was hot. He reached up under the fabric until he pulled it off over her head, letting it fall to the side on the balcony. She kissed him harder, teeth crashing against his, and knotted her fingers into fists in his hair. He pressed his fingers into her back before unclasping her bra. She shrugged out of it and let the stars and the moon shine down on her nakedness.

Desperate, she fumbled with his pants to free him. His cock was already hard, and she suspected it had been the minute she turned around and kissed him. She needed him. It felt like too much distance had grown between them in the days of working on his cure after the failure of their first attempt. She feared what may await them in the future if they lingered here too long. The Coven might find them, or other vampires who caught wind that there were foreigners in the old ruins of the 1500s house. She and Max might have been able to put up a good fight, but she and Julian were a totally different story.

She couldn't lose him.

She nipped at his bottom lip once she had him free of his pants. She slid forward in his lap until she felt him press against her. He gripped her ass and pushed her down on his length. A little gasp fell from her lips, and he growled as he filled her up.

She rocked in his lap, grinding on him, and he held on to her like he feared she might fall off the balcony and out of his life forever. She teased him with her fangs, grazing them over the smooth, unblemished skin of his neck. Goosebumps rose in her wake.

"Do it," he managed, voice grating as he thrust inside her.

"I won't take too much. You need your strength."

"Take as much as you want." He tipped his head back, baring his throat to her, and she sank her fangs into him.

His blood washed away the aftertaste of her feed earlier in the night. He was sweet, and clean, and so distinctly Julian.

As soon as his blood filled her mouth more flashes of Max's memories danced in her mind's eye. She watched herself from hundreds of years ago flee across a meadow of tall grass as he gave chase. Their laughter filled her ears in unison with Julian's moans and deep breathing. He held her tighter and drove in deeper. She purred his name against his throat, letting some of his blood dribble free so she could stop feeding and lick it up.

He shuddered, and she drew his face down into her cleavage as she rose and fell on his length. He held her tighter, and all at once, they both broke and gave in to the pleasure. He filled her up, and she let her head hang back and closed her eyes, remembering that day in the field with Max, and how once he'd caught her, he'd dragged her to the earth, tore her up, discarded her clothes, and made fierce love to her.

Love like this.

"Julian," she purred, sliding back down so she could lap at his blood.

He kissed her bloodied lips. "Ellie."

CHAPTER TWENTY-EIGHT

Ellie woke and felt off.

This had been happening every other day or so for the past couple of weeks. At first, she dismissed it as a side effect of not feeding as much as she should, but now that she'd rectified that situation, she could no longer chalk it up to that. Something in this eternal body of hers was new and foreign—something that did not belong. But she couldn't put her finger on what it was.

She frowned and blinked in the darkness of the lab. Julian slept soundly beside her, she could tell by his deep, steady breathing. She sat up, letting the blankets fall away, and rose from the bed in a fluid motion.

It wasn't as late as usual. She could feel that the sun had not yet set.

Why was she awake?

Somewhere outside, a bird chirped. Her ears pricked to the sound she wasn't used to hearing, and she paced to the trapdoor, straining to listen as more birds sang to each other as the day fell into night. She eyed Julian as he slept and waited, perfectly still beneath the trapdoor, for the sun to set some twenty minutes later. She shouldered the door open and stepped out into the early evening. The sun had set, and no rays touched her skin, but the sky was still bright with the lingering daylight.

She had never stood outside this early before.

She'd wondered over it for decades—centuries. But she'd always been holed up somewhere because that was how her kind survived. Back in the days of the Coven, she and Max would always find themselves a dark place to hunker down for the day, or they would join the others in their caves in the Spanish countryside. That lasted a long time before they began to build their own compound of sorts. It had been a risk. Hunters had eyes for such things. The manor had been the answer to all of their worries. It stood tall and proud and very human-looking. Passersby would assume Max and Eleonor were but simple country folk who preferred the quiet life of the hills and the trees over the bustle of town. And that was true, minus the simple folk part.

Ellie's uncertainty over what was happening to her shifted into unease as she gazed out at the light-tainted sky. Not even a single star had appeared yet, it was still too bright.

She felt a tremor inside of her and wondered what was going on, and if something was wrong. She and Julian had been working tirelessly on the cure, and she thought that maybe it was finally taking a toll. But that didn't make sense. Vampires didn't feel fatigue or sickness like humans. They were immune to it. Sure, they felt starvation and bloodlust, and a vampire who hadn't fed in a long time might genuinely feel ill in some capacity, but it was more a loss of control than anything else. This wasn't that. She'd fed recently enough. All her basic needs were met.

The tremor came again, and without thinking, she put her hand on her stomach.

The tremor felt like a pulse—like the one she was so used to kissing on Julian's neck. Steady and quick.

It couldn't be real.

She wrenched her hand away and stared down at her stomach. The only movement she had ever felt inside of herself since she'd been turned had been the stretching and swelling in her gut when she fed too much.

This was not that.

The flutter came again, and Ellie instinctively took a few steps back, as if she could run from the feeling. She could not. It followed her until she backed up against the stone of the fireplace. Gingerly, she returned her hand to her stomach and pressed firmly. Nothing came.

Sighing, she slumped against the stones.

She must have been losing her mind. All this razor focus on finding the cure had jumbled her brain. That must be it.

As she shook her head and dismissed the unease, the feeling came again, stronger this time, rippling through her like it was screaming for her attention. She gasped and clung to the stone, certain this time of what she'd felt: the ghost of a beating heart inside of her.

Ellie rushed to the trapdoor, wrenched it up, and hollered down to Julian that she was going to hunt, and she would return soon. He called up, voice full of fatigue, for her to be careful, but she'd already dropped the trapdoor and started running.

This is crazy, Ellie thought as she stood in the shadows of a closed-up bakery. She'd bided her time before coming into town, just like last time. The humans were all slumbering for the most part, minus the drunks and the youths who were still out and about looking for the final places willing to pour them a pint or a shot. They minded Ellie well enough alone. Nobody was interested in her purpose tonight.

Across the street, her target. A doctor's clinic. A sign in the window read *Daily Walk-Ins Welcome*, and there was a large red cross painted on the front window. The blinds were closed, and all the interior lights were off. A good thing, too. That way Ellie could move freely inside without her motion being detected from out on the street.

She waited until the area was silent and she couldn't hear any nearby humans before breaking in. Like the tanning salon, she used the back door. It was bolted from the inside, but she made short work of that, applying pressure to the door until the bolt bent like butter and eventually gave way with a groan and then a snap. She ducked inside, pressed the door closed, and turned to face the back room.

It smelled awfully sterile, and sterile it was. Every surface would have glistened if the lights were on. A doctor who cared thoroughly about his practice, that was for sure. She had no intention of messing up his stuff. She would leave everything intact. He would be dismayed when he saw the deadbolt and confused when he discovered nothing had been taken.

She only needed a couple of minutes here.

Ellie slipped down the dark hall, illuminated by the glare of a red EXIT sign. She ducked into the first examination room and used her night vision to seek out what she was here for, a stethoscope hanging on the wall beside a variety of other tools like an ear thermometer, flashlight, and blood pressure band.

She pulled the stethoscope from the wall, put it in her ears, and hovered the chest piece over the right side of her chest. She hesitated pressing it to herself.

What if she heard something?

What if she *didn't* hear something?

There was no plausible reason why she should have suddenly developed a heartbeat. No scientific explanation could justify why after all this time her heart had begun to beat again, but if Max could be reincarnated, could she not change back into the human she once was? A naïve, young, sweet, very much *alive* girl with a head full of dreams and a heart full of yearning for adventure? She got her adventure all right, but it hadn't been the one she wanted.

She bit down on the inside of her cheek until she tasted blood.

Ellie hadn't felt true fear in a very, very long time, but that was what this feeling was deep inside of her. She felt like she stood on the edge of a cliff, staring into the expanse of the dark unknown before her. There were no answers out there.

"Just do it." She pressed the chest piece to her chest and listened.

And listened.

And listened.

Nothing.

Silence. All that sat in her chest was a dead heart surrounded by dead tissue, muscle, and veins. She sighed, let the chest piece fall away, and leaned against the exam table.

"What did you expect?" she asked the room, shaking her head. Perhaps the fumes of Julian's cure were getting to her head.

Suddenly, it happened again. The flutter coursed through her, and without thinking, she pressed the chest piece to her stomach, and it happened.

She heard it.

That was not the ghost of a heartbeat. That was a real, fast, steady, rhythmic heartbeat. But it wasn't in her chest. It was in her *belly.*

"How?" she whispered, dropping the stethoscope. She dragged the fabric of her dress up, exposing her pale stomach, and grabbed it with both hands. She squeezed, as if she could feel what was inside of her. She felt normal. The same. Firm and thin and riddled with muscle.

It couldn't be.

A rush of panic swept over her only to be replaced by a desperate, furious need to feed. She wasn't sure where the desire came from, but she wondered if her instincts were taking over and her body was demanding blood because she was drinking for two now.

She rushed out of the doctor's office and began the hunt.

Her senses were keen and sharp, but her mind wandered down every path of questions. She shouldn't have been able to get pregnant, but here she was with a baby's heartbeat in her belly. Her and Julian's baby. None of it made sense.

She caught the scent of alcohol and blood and sought out the pulse of a man close by. She knew she shouldn't hunt in town, but she couldn't dismiss the need coursing through her. She had to feed, and she had to feed now.

She happened upon the man in a dark lane taking a piss against the side of someone's house. He pulled his phone out. The blinding light of the screen lit up his sneer as he started texting.

Ellie pulled herself up the side of the house and crept across the shingles of the roof, keeping low and choosing her steps carefully on all fours. She hovered over him and peered down at his phone screen. She knew instantly what this man was and thanked her lucky stars for finding the disgusting bastard when she was this hungry. If she'd gone too long, she worried she might have killed one of the good ones out of bloodlust.

He was texting a young teenager through a fake online profile. Once he was done, he switched to another one and did the same thing before scrolling through the girl's photos.

His little pastime was over.

Ellie dropped down from the roof like a bird of prey. The whooshing of her dress drew his attention upward just before she landed on him. She smothered his cry of surprise by clamping a hand over his mouth, and the rage inside of her tempted her to break his neck, but she wouldn't be able to feed on his blood then. So she slammed him up against the side of the house instead.

His phone smashed to pieces in his hand, the glass screen making a mess of his palm. The scent of his blood filled the air and made Ellie feel drunk with hunger. He slid to the ground, dazed, and she crouched down in front of him, grabbed his hand, pressed her nails into his wrist to draw more blood, and drank from him. He watched in horror as she pulled a liter of his blood into her mouth and swallowed. He never said a word. Never cried out. She held his gaze and kept him, paralyzed there until she was ready to consume all of him. She moved in, grabbed his hair, twisted his head to the side, and feasted.

He squirmed, feet thrashing against the stone ground until he died.

Ellie sat back on her heels and found herself panting. She had never fed with such ferocity before. She looked up at the stars as she licked her lips and felt the soothing sensation of the man's blood filling her up. The desperation that had propelled her to him ebbed away, and she felt in control again.

"For a vampire who's supposed to be dead, that was pretty brazen of you."

Ellie stumbled back and got to her feet, spinning toward the shadows at the back of the house, where the figure of a man emerged, arms crossed over his chest, a familiar smirk playing on his lips. She narrowed her eyes, soaking in the sight of him. Long, brown hair drawn back off his shoulders, broad nose, lean, tall, and a blade in his belt.

His name dripped from her lips like venom. "Matteo."

CHAPTER TWENTY-NINE

"It's been a long time, Eleonor." Matteo moved a little closer, testing his limits with her. "Where the hell have you been all these years?"

"Traitor," she spat.

Matteo, ever the same sly, cocky, evasive bastard he'd always been, pressed his hands to his chest like he'd been unjustly accused. "Me? A traitor? You don't have your facts straight. Maybe all this time alone has turned your brain to mush." He lifted his chin and his lips turned down in a disapproving half-frown. "Not maybe. Definitely. I heard you hunting a quarter mile away and smelled his blood as soon as you broke his phone."

Ellie squared her shoulders. If she'd been human, she would have taken a deep breath to settle her anger, but she was not. The only calming technique she had was presence of mind and control. She un-balled her fists from her sides, softened her jaw, and swallowed the remnants of copper lingering on her tongue.

"I didn't think any of the Coven would still be here," she said.

He paced casually into the moonlight, and she followed suit.

He ignored her comment about the Coven. "You look almost the same."

She resisted the urge to say 'duh' and instead nodded. "As we all do."

Ellie had no idea if lesser vamps in the Coven like Matteo had any knowledge of her and Max's betrayal. For all she knew, he'd been just as in the dark as she was. But on the other hand, he might have been privy to information that could have saved Max's life, and hers by default. Either way, she couldn't trust him.

And either way, he'd made himself very accessible to her when she was having a hard time hunting vampires for Julian's experiments.

She forced herself to look passive, while deep inside, she chomped at the bit to attack. She was aware of the stake in her shoulder bag, pressing against her hip, tempting her to grab it and plunge it into his heart. He was leaving with her, or he was dying here. Those were her only two options. She couldn't risk him returning to whatever hole he'd crawled out of and spilling the truth to the rest of the remaining Coven that she was still alive.

"Aren't you bored of the same old towns?" she asked.

Matteo shrugged. "I don't believe I experience boredom. You'll understand when you get older."

Condescending ass.

Only a few feet away now, she peered up at him, feigning curiosity. "How old are you now? Three millennia?"

"Watch your tongue, Eleonor de León. Two millennia."

She forced herself to laugh even though the sound of her old name had rattled her. She hadn't heard it in a long time, and it stirred up old resentments, wishes, and dreams.

She looked over her shoulder at the dead man in an attempt to draw his attention. "If I'd known you were coming, I'd have saved you a drop or two."

His gaze flicked past her to the corpse. "I prefer my meals packaged in dresses and high heels." He sneered. "But thank you for the hindsight consideration."

Matteo had always been full of jokes, even back then. He and Max had once been something close to friends until he made a pass at Eleonor one night on a group hunt that she shot down and he wouldn't accept as an answer. He resented monogamy and thought it blasphemy in the realms of their Coven and immortal beings. He believed that sex and blood should be shared, as all things should be shared, and he'd wanted her more than he wanted anything.

He and Max had come to fights more than once, and Ellie had been privy to them. She recalled how he fought—he was precise, quick, and way too cocky. Matteo always thought he had the win in the bag before Max pulled one over on him.

She could do the same right here, right now.

Matteo pursed his lips and looked her over. "Speaking of dresses..."

She saw her moment and pounced, pulling her stake out of her bag in one fluid motion as she surged forward, low and quick, her aim true. Matteo tried to smack her hand away as he leapt back in retreat, but she'd anticipated his escape route based on how he'd been standing with his left foot back, right foot slightly forward. He stepped back with his right to create more space, but she followed, ducked under the reach of his arm, and drove the stake straight up through his ribs and into his heart.

A pitiful yelp escaped him before he slumped forward, all his weight falling on her. She pressed her shoulder under his chest as his black blood seeped across her skin and into her hair. She should have tied it up.

"Bitch," he breathed before passing out, his knees buckling beneath him.

She grabbed him by his belt, plucked his blade free to tuck

into her own bag, and hauled him over her shoulder. "Two millennia is long enough for a stain like you to be alive."

ELLIE THREW Matteo down the trapdoor. He landed face-first on the dirt.

Julian leapt back with a startled cry. She jumped down the stairs, landing in a crouch beside the unconscious vampire.

Julian rushed to her and pulled her into him. "You were gone a long time. Are you okay?"

She pushed him gently away. "I'm covered in blood."

"I don't care." He pulled her back in, and she let him.

She breathed in his musk and the smells of the lab. He'd definitely been working on something down here all night.

When they parted, he looked down at Matteo. "What's this?"

She rolled the vampire over and used her foot to turn his face to Julian. "Recognize him?"

At first, Julian just shrugged, but then his gaze darkened and his lips pressed together in a fine line. "Matteo."

"Mhm. Matteo. Rogue member of the Coven, predator of young women in the valley, and altogether slimeball." She looked up at him. "And your next test subject."

Julian grabbed her hand and pulled her to the far corner of the lab. "This was risky, Ellie! He's a Coven member! I thought this was exactly what we were trying to avoid!" He raked his fingers through his hair, leaving it sticking up every which way. "What if they notice he's gone?"

"Back when we were Coven members, Matteo would leave the group for weeks, sometimes months at a time. And he was never missed. Do you think anything has changed, or do you think he's become even more unlikeable?"

Julian scratched his chin. His skin was stained with grit and dirt. "Fair point."

"Besides," she added under her breath, "he caught me with

my defenses down while I was feeding, and I couldn't let him leave. My hands were tied. Now let's tie his."

Together, Julian and Ellie got Matteo bound in one of the storage rooms of the manor. The cure wasn't ready to test yet. Julian said he needed another night, maybe two or three. Ellie didn't like the sound of that, but she had no choice but to be patient. If the sample wasn't ready, it wasn't ready.

They bound Matteo with silver wire and chains and shone one of the spare UV lights at him. It would simulate daylight, which, along with the stake in his chest, would keep him asleep indefinitely until they were ready to conduct their next test. Once they were confident he wasn't going to escape, they closed the storage door and retreated upstairs to enjoy the final hour of the night together.

Instead of going up to the balcony, as per their usual ritual, they went out to the front of the manor and sat on the grass as it began collecting dew. Julian told her all about his night and his cure, and all the things he'd done differently, and she noticed the cadence of confidence in his tone as it rose and fell with excitement.

She bided her own enthusiasm. She'd been disappointed before, and she had to manage her expectations.

Especially now that there was this life beating inside of her.

She wanted to tell Julian desperately, but she feared it would be a mistake. He already had so much on his plate. He already wasn't sleeping. He'd lost weight. He tossed and turned in the night. He felt the heavy burden of trying to rescue her from her own immortality. She couldn't add another thing to that list, especially with all the unknown it brought with it.

In all her years of research and scouring books on vampires, she had never come across a case or even a mention of one getting pregnant. It simply wasn't possible. A baby needed a living mother to host it—coursing blood, passing of nutrients, and the ability to grow a placenta and an umbilical cord. How could Ellie do any of that when she was dead? Deep down, she suspected this wasn't going to come to fruition, and she would bear the heartbreak alone and spare Julian.

She had already lost enough in all these years. She knew perfectly well how to deal with grief and pain. She could do it again.

Julian wrapped his arms around her. "What are you thinking about?"

"Nothing," she answered a little too quickly.

They were both quiet for a moment, and she hoped he would leave it alone.

He didn't. "Are you sure you're okay with this?"

"What?"

"Testing the cure on Matteo. Once upon a time, we were all friends."

"I'm sure."

He nodded. "Three nights, and we'll test it. I have a good feeling about this one, Ellie. It might just be the one that sticks. All this work, all this time… I think it's going to pay off. I think I'm going to be able to save you."

"Oh, Julian." She turned to him and knelt on the grass as the sky lightened above their heads, shifting from black, to navy, to a hue of purple as the sun crept closer to breaking the horizon. "You already saved me."

She pulled him in to kiss him.

He wrapped her up and rolled her over, pinning her beneath him in the grass. Moisture seeped into her dress as she slid her hands up his shirt, feeling his abs and chest muscles beneath her cold skin. Hurriedly, she shimmied her dress up, revealing she wasn't wearing underwear. She hadn't in days. She hadn't packed enough, and it was unnecessary really. Julian growled in appreciation.

Ellie needed him *now*. No waiting. No teasing.

She tore his pants open. The seams ripped. He scowled and

pouted over her ruining his favorite pants but shut up when she lifted his hips and guided her deep inside her. A soft moan escaped his perfect lips, and she drew him down to her to devour his mouth while she rolled her hips and felt him press into all the most delicious places inside her.

The sky continued to lighten overhead.

She moaned in his ear as he held her down in the grass and drove deeper inside of her. Something felt different, and she was reminded of the little life growing inside of her. Was that why she'd been so turned on so fast?

"Harder," she demanded.

Make me forget all our worries.

He thrust deep inside her, and both of them reached their climax as the sun painted the skyline orange. She felt warmth on her skin for the first time in centuries, and Julian quickly blocked it out with his own body, casting her into shadow beneath him as he came inside her with a shudder and a growl. She clung to him, aching to stay like this forever, feeling the day warm up around her but staying protected in his shadow.

"Let's get you inside," he said.

He used his size to protect her, and before stepping into the manor, Ellie reached two fingers to the side, letting the rising sun kiss her skin. It burned, but not the way it used to.

CHAPTER THIRTY

Ellie had been growing restless with every nightfall. She wanted to get this over with with Matteo. He'd regained consciousness the second night they had him, and he'd growled through the storage room door, threatening them that if they didn't let him go, the Coven would find them and destroy them.

Again.

Julian didn't seem at all bothered by this. He told her it was just a desperate vampire grasping at straws and doing whatever he could to con them into letting him go. She knew that too, deep down, but still, there was a part of her that had begun to fret. There was a living *thing* inside of her, a secret she hadn't let Julian in on, and parts of her were changing.

She was hungry all the time.

The sun, if it was far enough away, did not weaken her the way it used to.

Her patience was slipping.

She felt strange. She didn't like not having control of what was happening to her, and not having control in their daily life wasn't helping. She wished there was some way she could take the reins, but all she could do was hunt and wait while Julian worked away on his cure and Matteo spat curses from behind the storage room door.

It was maddening.

Especially when the third night passed and the cure was not ready like Julian had hoped. So, while he worked, she sat in front of the door while Matteo slumbered. Every now and then she heard him begin to stir, but he never fully woke under the UV light and the other precautions they'd taken. Julian told her she should go hunt or get some fresh air—pointless for a vampire—or do something to pass the hours.

She decided to go into the storage room. Julian didn't like it, but he was too distracted by his work to stop her. She stepped inside and shielded her eyes against the glare of the UV light. Matteo's skin had purpled under it, and for a brief second, she felt a twinge of guilt.

She resented the human emotion, pushed it down, and turned the light off.

Matteo, slumped in the chair to which he was bound, came to in the passing minutes, and murmured a messy thank you to her. She hadn't done it for him, she told herself. She'd done it so she could sit cross-legged on the dirt floor in front of him.

"What are you going to do with me?" Matteo asked when he gathered his wits. His voice was thin and wavery.

"Kill you, probably."

He snorted. "After holding me for four nights? Why?"

She told him that if he answered some of her questions, maybe she would answer his, which was a flat-out lie. But he agreed and nodded for her to ask anyway. She started off with questions that didn't matter just to warm him up and get him talking. He was half-delirious, and his time under the light with the stake in his chest scrambled his head. He was not of the presence of mind to lie, and if he tried, she would know.

Finally, she worked her way to what she actually wanted to know.

"What happened the night Max was killed? Who gave the order?" She leaned forward, desperate for answers she'd only ever wondered about.

Matteo grimaced. "It was messy, Eleonor. Really messy, and it wasn't supposed to be. Your father... his regret never ended."

"Did he give the order?"

Matteo eyed her. "Yes."

If she'd been human, the hair on the back of her neck might have stood up. As it were, her insides boiled. "Why?"

"It was never about you," Matteo explained. "You were just caught in the crossfire."

"So it was about Max?"

The weakened vampire nodded. "Your father found out that Max was working on a cure to rid us of our vampiric nature. Some of us were curious, but he was threatened. He spread word to the elders, who discussed for weeks how they should handle the issue before deciding that Max had to be stopped by whatever means necessary. Your father knew him well enough to know that even if they destroyed his work, his lab, his notes, all of it, Max would begin anew. He had to die."

Eleonor waited for him to continue. When he didn't, she nudged him. "And?"

"And so he arranged the attack. Most of the Coven didn't know about it. I didn't know until years later," he added, probably for personal gain to get her to erase his name from her ledger. Not going to happen. "He made plans to leak the location of the manor to a local vampire-hunting troupe in the area. Once they caught wind, and your father knew they were on Max's trail, he arranged to go hunting with you that night so you wouldn't be home when they came for Max. But you changed your mind last minute, and your father was bound by an agreement with the council not to intervene. He had said by whatever means necessary, and when you put yourself in the crossfire, there was nothing he could do to save you."

"He chose power over his daughter," she hissed. "He chose to betray me. He could have chosen to betray them. But he did not. Don't defend him."

Matteo didn't meet her gaze. "None of the Coven wanted you dead, Eleonor. You were well-loved. So was Max, by most. But his experiments were traitorous and blasphemous. You have to understand that he couldn't be allowed to proceed. His work presented a bigger threat to our kind than the hunters who wanted to burn us. It was self-preservation, nothing more."

"I wanted it," she whispered.

Matteo fought to keep his eyes open. The black blood around the stake protruding from his chest had long since dried. He needed to feed to regain his strength, but his days of drinking human blood were over. "Wanted what?"

"The cure," she said. "I don't want to be this. I don't want to kill people. I don't want an eternal life. And I was cursed to live one without the man I loved, because why? Because my father and a bunch of crusty, old elders thought that Max would force his cure on them? That wasn't the plan! All Max wanted was to offer a way out to those who didn't choose this life, and who didn't want it. He was giving them a chance to go back to a normal life. Back to sunrises and *food*. Don't you ever miss real food? I can't even remember what anything tastes like. Not really. The smell of fresh-baked bread used to rise me from my bed in the mornings, and now it makes my stomach churn. All Max wanted was to hand us a *choice*."

Matteo licked his dry, cracking lips. "He was committing a sin."

"We commit a sin just by existing." She got to her feet and jabbed a finger at him. "How many lives have you taken to sustain your own? How many families have you broken?"

"We are superior," he growled.

She shook her head and laughed bitterly. Superior. No. In all her long years, she had learned that vampires were not the all-knowing, wondrous creatures her father had led her to believe. They were tragedies. Deadly ones. They were cursed to roam the earth, feeding on the innocent until eventually there was nothing left.

"Every human I bled dry should be grateful their blood sustained me," Matteo managed through clenched teeth. His fatigue settled deep into his hollow cheeks and the sunken flesh beneath his eyes. He'd been handsome when she first ran into him in town. Now he looked like the monster they both were. "They should be honored! A life like mine cannot be compared to the fleeting lives of a human. What do they know of the world? They're here for a flash of time and they are as insignificant as they are wretched. Selfish. Pitiful."

"They rule this world," she reminded him. "We do not. We live in shadows and caves. We *hide*. If we were so worthy of a life on this planet, don't you think it would be easier?"

He scoffed. "Easy does not equal worth. You always were weak. Your father sensed it in you. He knew you weren't cut out for the long-sustained life of an elder. He made peace with the fact that he would outlive you long before they cut Max's head from his shoulders and burned him on that pyre like he deserved!"

Her temper flared. "You will not be so lucky to die a quick death, Matteo."

Just then, Julian knocked on the door and pushed it open. It creaked on old hinges and came to a stop. He looked from her to Matteo, and back to her.

"It's done," he said.

Ellie straightened. "You're sure?"

He nodded once. "Get him on the slab."

Matteo stiffened. "What? What are you two doing?"

Ellie turned to him, that same uncontrollable need to spill

his blood rippling through her like it did the night she killed the man on his cell phone. She felt her lips peel off her teeth in a smile, flashing fangs, and grabbed the back of Matteo's chair. She hauled him out of the storage room. The legs of the chair growled against the dirt floor. Matteo thrashed so wildly he almost tipped himself over as she prepared the chains on the table. She lifted him, still bound, and placed him on the slab before tying him down. The stake in his chest still rendered him relatively useless, but his panic had resorted some movement.

"Let me go," he pleaded. "Show me mercy."

"Like the Coven showed Max mercy?" she asked.

Memories of the night she lost Max came back to her. She could almost feel his coldness pressed up against her in the back of that wagon as they were brought to their fate in the center of that old town. She heard him ask her over and over for her to run, and heard herself finally promise that she would.

She felt the echoes of agony rip through her as she remembered how they had beaten him before they decapitated him, and how she'd watched his blood spill free before they threw him onto the fire, not leaving anything for her to come back for and bury if she'd been able to.

Not letting her say goodbye.

After chasing vengeance for so long, she couldn't believe she was this close. A Coven member lay before her, begging for his life with so little dignity compared to how Max had faced his demise. And Matteo thought he was superior. Not on his life. He was weak, and fragile, and shallow, and he deserved this.

They all did.

Julian went about preparing his vials while she tuned out the sounds of Matteo's begging. She recalled how hard she'd run that night with tears streaming down her face, and how she'd clung to those words Max used to say to her when the days and nights felt heavier than normal.

Hope dies last.

She put a hand to her stomach.

Was this what hope felt like? She'd thought she felt it before now that Julian was back in her life, but after the failed tests with the cure, and all this aimless waiting, she'd lost it. But now, with this little heartbeat inside of her, and her building fear—something she hadn't felt in ages—she remembered this feeling.

Hope.

True, unabashed, shameless *hope*.

She'd felt it when she and Max first broke ground on the manor, and again when he kissed her and told her he loved her for the first time. She'd felt it when he promised her a life in the manor, either an eternal one or a mortal one, and it had soared within her when he started working on his cure for the first time. In her lonely, wandering years between Max and Julian, she had accepted that she would never feel hopeful again.

But reincarnation had given her a second chance, and perhaps all of her suffering would be rewarded with what she and Max had wanted more than anything else, and the main reason why they'd pursued the cure in the first place.

A child.

CHAPTER THIRTY-ONE

Matteo was begging, and it was getting pathetic.

Ellie tried to tune him out as Julian continued preparations, but his voice was grating, and the more desperate he became, the higher the pitch in his voice grew. It itched at her insides until she couldn't stand it anymore.

She stormed over to Julian. "How can I help?"

"Almost ready." He pinched his tongue between his lips as he drew the cure from the vial into a syringe, just like he had on the last vampire they tested.

Murdered.

Whatever.

Ellie watched as the syringe filled, and Matteo managed to twist his head around on the slab as she and Julian approached him. His eyes fixed on the syringe, and he went stiff.

"This is what you and your little human henchman have been doing?" He strained viciously against the chains. The metal grated against the stone slab, but not even he had the force required to break free of their holy water-soaked confines. He strained until his eyeballs looked like they were going to pop out of his head before settling back down in exhaustion. If the stake wasn't still in his heart, Ellie knew Matteo might have escaped. He'd always been one of the strong ones.

And clearly, Matteo had no idea that Julian was Max reincarnated. A human henchman? Nonsense. Ellie wouldn't have been caught dead letting a human do her dirty work. This was different. This was her long, lost lover.

This was justice.

Ellie and Julian ignored him, and she had to fight him to turn his arm over, exposing the inside of his elbow and the dark veins standing out against his pale skin.

Matteo looked from the syringe to Ellie. "Don't do this. This is a mistake! I can help you. I can report back to the Coven that I confirmed you are actually dead. I can—"

"Enough," Ellie said.

"I'll do whatever you want!"

For a 'superior being,' in his words, Matteo was showing an unsightly, cowardly side of himself. She'd seen humans go to their deaths with better grace than him, and they'd only had three decades of life, not two millennia.

He should be grateful he had that long.

"Have some dignity," Ellie said as she took the syringe from Julian. He relinquished it to her and stared grimly down at their next victim.

Neither of them had any idea if this would actually work. Julian hoped, and Ellie was cautiously optimistic, but there was no indication it would go the way they wanted.

She held the syringe up in front of her eyes and inspected the liquid. It looked even clearer than the last time.

"What did you do differently?" she asked.

Julian studied the contents of the needle beside her, hovering just over her shoulder. "The UV lamp and the way it incapacitated Matteo inspired me. I wondered if it incapacitated him because it stripped him of some of his abilities, so I cured the cure"—he paused for a cocky smirk at his little pun—"under the light for twenty-four hours. And I added my own blood."

She marveled at the liquid. If he'd added his own blood, why wasn't it red? It remained clear, almost like water, but thicker, like an oil.

"Tell me that's not what I think it is," Matteo said. "Tell me you haven't spent all this time trying to recreate Max's cure."

She wiggled the syringe in front of him. "Clever you."

He bared his fangs and snapped at the air.

Julian flinched, but Ellie held fast. She wasn't afraid of a bound vampire, and they were too close now to be deterred by sharp teeth when she had a set of her own.

For now.

She hovered the point of the needle over his arm. Julian crossed his fingers and pressed them to his temples, muttering aloud over and over that this *had* to work this time. Matteo begged and pleaded. She guided the needlepoint into his vein. His muscles flexed as he tried desperately to break free, but as the cure filled his veins and began coursing through him, all the fight went out of him.

His brows drew together in dismay. "No, no, no. *No*!"

Eleonor stumbled back, and Julian leaned forward, curiosity getting the better of him. She grabbed the back of his shirt and pulled him back.

Suddenly, Matteo let out a shriek of sound that was far from being human or vampire. It tore out of him, and he went silent just as quickly. His head thrashed from side to side, and Ellie's gaze went to the stake in his chest. She waited for the blood to bubble like it had with the last vamp.

He seized. His whole body shook so vigorously that his teeth chattered in his skull.

The lab flooded with the scent of blood.

Human blood.

Ellie grabbed Julian's hand. He let out a startled yelp when she squeezed too hard, and she lifted his knuckles to her lips and kissed them in silent apology. She couldn't tear her eyes off the sight before her. Matteo writhed and let out one last pitiful scream before he began choking on black blood and gore that spilled out of his mouth like vomit.

Then he fell still.

The scent of human blood lingered.

Ellie waited. Julian's heart thundered in his chest.

Everything remained perfectly still.

Julian deflated. "I thought I had it. I thought that was it. Shit!" He wound back and kicked a bunch of lab items near his table. They scattered across the dirt with a clash.

Ellie's hand fell to her stomach and the small heartbeat there. Was it a good thing that the cure had failed once more? Would she even be able to take it, and if she did, what would it cost her? She'd learned in all these years that nothing came for free—especially things she'd wanted for such a long time. If the cure killed the baby, would it be worth it? Would she give up mortality in order to give Julian a child?

Yes.

Could she endure an ageless life while both her lover and her child grew old, withered, and died before her eyes?

The pang of loneliness that hit her almost pushed her into oblivion.

She stumbled toward the slab and gripped the edge.

Julian paced the ground behind her. "I don't understand what I did wrong. I thought this was it. Maybe I need to use sunlight instead of UV light. Maybe the simulation is what spoiled it. I'm sorry, Ellie. I'm so sorry."

She tightened her hold on the slab. The stone did not feel like stone at all in her grip. It felt like a tree trunk, supple enough for her to break if she applied enough pressure.

"I'll try again." Julian came up behind her and put a hand on her shoulder. "I'll try again."

She shook her head. "Maybe this isn't how things are supposed to be, Julian. Maybe we're fighting against nature too hard. Maybe... maybe it's time to accept what we cannot change and embrace what we already have." Once more, her hand went to her stomach.

"I'm not ready to walk away."

What if I am? she thought.

He gave her shoulder a squeeze. "Give me one more try. Let me cure it in sunlight and see what happens. I think I have all the right ingredients, it's just a matter of finesse. Capturing the right elements. Hope dies—"

"Don't." She turned to him, vision blurring with tears. "I can't be strung along by hope any longer. I have been waiting for almost three hundred years, Julian. I don't want to wait anymore, or fight, or run, I just want to *be*. Please. Let me be."

She saw the heartbreak in his eyes. "But... but you'll be like this forever."

"One lifetime with you will be worth it."

It has to be.

Julian took her by the shoulders. She watched as he struggled to find the right thing to say, but she knew there was no right thing. She waited anyway, feeling his agony seeping off of him until all of a sudden, he straightened and pulled her aside.

"Look," Julian breathed.

She followed to where he was pointing—to the stake in Matteo's chest.

The blood had turned red.

She inched closer, reached out, and swept her finger through it. She sniffed it. "Human," she said, before licking it. "Entirely human."

Without thinking, she pulled the stake out of Matteo's chest.

Blood poured out of the wound, but it closed before their very eyes, and suddenly Matteo drew a wet, messy breath, coughed, and spat black clumps onto the ground. He took deep breaths—the first breaths he'd drawn in a very long time—and looked around wildly until he spotted Ellie.

"What have you done to me?" he whispered.

CHAPTER THIRTY-TWO

Julian leaned over the table, inspecting Matteo like the lab rat he was. "It worked. I can't believe it worked. All this time… all this work…"

"It wasn't for nothing," Ellie finished for him.

She'd been there through almost all of those hours of work, the sleepless nights, the frustration, and the crippling disappointment after each failure. She couldn't even define the feeling coursing through her. She was excited and frightened all at once. She couldn't help but wonder if that all had to do with the baby in her stomach. *If* she wasn't pregnant, she probably would have told Julian to inject her right here, right now, and get all the anticipation over with.

Matteo, however, did not seem conflicted.

His rage was evident as he glared up at them. "Unbind me," he seethed. "You ruined me! You ruined everything! How dare you!" The fire went out of him after some pathetic straining. Now that he didn't have his vampiric strength, Ellie felt almost embarrassed for him as he strained, turned bright red, and gave up. His voice sounded like the hollow shell of the vampire he used to be. "I'm nothing now."

"You're a miracle," Julian breathed. "A living, breathing human after thousands of years on earth. It's possible. Don't you understand what this means?"

"It means my days are numbered," Matteo hissed, "all so you could prove yourself right."

Julian shook his head. "You're missing the point. It means every wandering vampire who is withering away into nothingness from this life can come back to who they used to be, even if just for a short time, before they die. Before they get to leave. It's natural to die, Matteo. We're not supposed to walk the earth for thousands of years."

"I hate philosophers," Matteo said.

Ellie wrapped her arms around herself. While Julian talked excitedly with Matteo, who she knew would not be convinced, she became aware of what she had to do.

"Do you still need him for more experiments?" Ellie asked.

Julian looked over at her like he'd forgotten she was there. "Not really, I suppose. We can release him. Just think, Matteo. You can walk in the sunlight. You can go into town and order a French onion soup, or drink a beer, or—"

"I want none of those simple things," Matteo spat, but his stomach grumbled, defying his words.

"You can make the most of this," Julian said.

Ellie moved to stand beside Julian and stared down at Matteo. A long, long time ago, she used to consider him a friend. She'd known him longer than she knew Max. They'd hunted together, fed together, and snuck away from the Coven together to practice their combat skills without the watchful eye of their instructors on them all the time. Yes, they'd been friends. She wasn't sure who'd been different back then, her, or Matteo.

Probably both of them.

In her memories, he seemed so much softer. He'd cared about things other than himself. Yes, he'd always been a bit blood-crazy, but that was a common quality amongst vampires, especially back then. All these years had darkened his mind even more.

What did that say about the rest of the Coven? What dark deeds had they done since arranging Max's murder? Did they still use humans to do their dirty work to commit sin against their own kind? Who was worse, she and Julian for changing Matteo against his will, or the Coven for bleeding their own members?

She decided it didn't matter.

Julian reached for the chains to release Matteo, who had crumpled beneath the realization of his new existence.

"I can never go back," he said. "The Coven will never take me like this. They'll destroy me. My family… they will turn against me."

"Join the club," Ellie said dryly.

Matteo's eyes slid to her. "Please."

Julian frowned back and forth between them.

She knew what Matteo was asking for, and she had every intention of giving it to him had he asked or not. Without hesitation, she reached down, took both sides of his head in her hands, and twisted sharply. His neck snapped with a series of loud cracks, and he went still on the table.

Julian exclaimed in surprise and stumbled back from the table. "Ellie! What have you done?"

"What he wanted me to do," she said simply. "His life was over. The Coven would never take him back. We sentenced him to live his final days as I've lived my last three hundred years. In isolation. Besides," she added, letting her hands fall to her sides, "we couldn't risk word of our successful experiment getting out. Matteo is still part of the Coven, and if he decided to seek vengeance on us, I have no doubt he would sacrifice himself in order to tell the others what we've done. They killed you once for this. I won't let that happen again."

Julian stared at the corpse.

Ellie took his hand and guided him to the corner of the lab, away from the blood and death. "Don't pity him."

"I know you're right," he whispered.

She took his face in her hands and forced him to look down at her. "Tell me what this means now."

His brow creased and he closed his hands over hers, engulfing her fingers with warmth from his palms. "It means the cure is ready. It means we're finally where we've been trying to go." He leaned down and rested his forehead against hers. He closed his eyes. She could have counted his eyelashes if she wanted to. She stared at the perspiration on his skin and his pores. If and when she turned back into a human, would she lose sight of tiny details of the man she loved? She would no longer be able to hear his heartbeat when she came home from a hunt before even opening the trapdoor. Would she miss that? Would it make her uneasy not to hear it? Julian's eyes fluttered open. "We can test more if you want."

She shook her head. "I don't want to do this again."

Julian looked relieved. "Me neither."

Ellie knew she was standing in the moment where she should tell him about the baby, but she couldn't make the words come out of her. She felt paralyzed by all the unknown. Any decision she made right now could easily be the wrong one.

Julian pulled her in close. "Tell me what you need."

She stood in the circle of his arms. She hadn't expected to feel this way. She thought when he finally succeeded that she would finally feel… she didn't know… free? Excited? Relieved? Joyful?

She felt none of those things.

"Do you still want this?" he whispered.

She held him tighter. Immortality meant condemning herself to more centuries without Julian. It meant raising this child without their father, if things went well with this pregnancy, which she doubted they could if she remained a vampire. Sooner or later, whatever little miracle had transpired to allow her to conceive would wear off. She suspected this had only been made possible due to her exposure to all the stuff in the lab, but for all she knew, she was wrong. There may never be answers to why this was all happening.

"I still want this," she said more to assure herself than answer him.

Remaining a vampire was not an option on the table, even though it might have felt easier and more familiar. They had done this together to pursue a future they both deserved. They'd killed for it. She didn't want to feed and take life anymore. She didn't want to be this way. An animal. She wanted to escape the heaviness of this life and begin anew by returning to the woman she used to be.

She and Julian could go back to New York. He could continue his studies, and she could, well…

Her thoughts wandered.

She'd never considered what she might want to do with her human life.

If all went well, she would carry her baby to full term and become a mother. Maybe she would raise them at home, in Julian's beautiful house, surrounded by books and sunlight and playdates at the park, along with all the other kids. She could make friends. Real, true, simple human friends. She could drink wine and celebrate holidays. She could learn how to cook.

She could get a job.

She had no idea where she'd start, but the thought appealed nonetheless.

Julian kissed the top of her head. "It will all be okay, Ellie. I've got you."

He must have been able to sense all of her apprehension. He and Max had always been able to read the depths of her thoughts, or at least feel the energy seeping out of her as she sifted through them.

"After all this time..." she breathed. "I just can't believe we've finally done it."

She felt a chuckle vibrate in his chest. "I can. We make a great team, you and me. And with you by my side, I can do anything."

"Even when I'm human?" She tipped her head back and stared up at him once more. "I won't be able to protect us, Julian. I'll be... weak. I'll need to sleep more. Eat more. Drink water," she added, almost appalled by the idea.

Julian laughed. "Yes, you will have to do all those things. But just think. On Sunday mornings you can sleep in as the sunlight breaks through the curtains, and I can go downstairs and make us coffee. Or tea. I'll bring it up to you. We can have a lazy start and walk to get scones at the café down my street. You'll love it, Ellie. *We'll* love it. I know it's scary, and it's a lot of change, but you don't have to start this new life on your own like you did last time. I'll be right there with you the whole time. I promise. This is our second chance at a life together. A normal, real, flawed, messy, human life."

She licked her lips. "There's no going back if we do it."

"We won't want to go back."

She nodded and looked down.

He placed two fingers under her chin and lifted her face. "You don't have to decide right this second. You have time. Whatever you decide, I support you. I can't imagine what it would be like to face this decision, and I understand that for a really long time, you probably believed you would never have to. I swear, Ellie, I have no expectations of you. I just want you to choose what is right for you."

"I love you," she whispered.

He pressed the softest, sweetest kiss to her lips she had ever felt. "I love you, too."

CHAPTER THIRTY-THREE

They decided to drag Matteo up out of the basement and bury him before they lost the darkness of night.

Ellie shoveled while Julian wrapped the corpse in a tarp and bound it with twine. They dug a few miles from the manor, and Ellie hoped it was far enough. If vampires or other predators sniffed him out, she didn't want the path to point immediately back to the manor.

Once the hole was dug, they lowered Matteo into it.

Julian wiped the sweat from his brow. "The bastard is heavy."

She smiled as she piled on dirt, trying to remember what fatigue and perspiration felt like. She could not. It had been too long.

"You're sure this is far enough from the manor?" Julian looked around, peering into the darkness of the surrounding trees.

He had nothing to worry about. There was nothing around for miles but owls and sleeping squirrels. She had her ears pricked, and her nose sniffed at the air every few seconds. If someone was coming, she would know it.

"For how long we're going to be there, yes." She finished

covering the grave and leaned on the shovel. "We can't stay here, Julian."

He arched an eyebrow. "You want to leave? But we were rebuilding. I thought we were going to make this our forever home. I thought we were starting over here." He frowned. "Does this mean you've decided not to take the cure? Do you want to go back to how things were in New York?"

She shook her head. "No, I have decided I want to take the cure. Tonight. And once I do, we won't be safe to stay here. We'll always be looking over our shoulders, wondering if the Coven is going to find us, and if they ever did, there would be nothing we could do to defend against them. I want a human life with you, Julian. And I want it in New York."

Julian skirted around the fresh dirt lumped on top of the grave and hurried to her. "You mean it?"

She nodded. Inside, she felt the faintest flutter of movement in her belly. She knew she wouldn't be able to feel it once she took the cure. That would stress her out. Right now, with her vampire senses, she had constant reassurance that the life inside of her was still, well, alive. Once she turned human, she would lose all of those supernatural perks and would be doomed to the unknowing all mothers faced.

Another reason to move back to New York?

Doctors.

As soon as she and Julian returned, she intended to make an appointment to make sure everything checked out. She had no idea how to show up or behave at a doctor's office, but she'd figure it out. She had to.

"I mean it," she said.

With a joyful laugh, Julian scooped her off the ground in his arms and twirled her in a circle. From the outside looking in, they would have looked like psychopaths kissing and dancing over a fresh grave.

"I don't want to wait anymore," she whispered. And she

didn't want to change her mind, either. "I'm ready. Let's go back to the manor. I want the cure."

Julian held her a little tighter.

She smelled his fear radiating off him.

"It will be okay," she assured him. "I have all the faith in the world that this will work."

He nodded grimly. "Suddenly the stakes feel very high."

She stroked his cheek. "I know."

He kissed her deeply as he set her down on the ground. His hands lingered on her lower back before slipping down to her rear end. He squeezed and pulled her hips against him. She felt him grow hard against her stomach and smiled against his lips.

"One last time before it all changes?" she cooed before peppering kisses down his neck.

Julian nuzzled her chin to the side to press kisses of her own across her shoulders. "One last time. But not here."

Julian laid her down on the balcony off of what might have once more been their bedroom on the second story of the manor. The stars twinkled overhead as he worked with slow, patient fingers to untie the lace front of her dress. She waited patiently, staring adoringly up at the man of her dreams and the expanse of stars behind him. She tried to capture every movement, sigh, and moment that passed between them as he got her dress undone and gently worked it off her body. She lay on top of it while he caressed the milky skin of her thighs as if he too worried she might feel different to him after she took the cure.

Would he still look and feel the same to her once she was human? She could never know until that time was upon them, which was why she felt the painful need to soak up every passing second.

Julian lay down beside her on the stone. Soon, she would feel just how cold that stone was, but not tonight.

He propped himself up on an elbow to hold himself over her as he kissed her like he might lose her. And he might. He was caught in the same place she was with Max in that wagon. She knew he was scared and that he had to put all his trust into his cure. After so many failures, and all this time, she could only imagine how terrified he was that it might not work on her.

She had made peace with the fact that this might be her last night alive—not that she considered herself alive right now. If this was how it all ended, so be it.

She cupped his cheek. "If this doesn't work, promise me you'll go back to New York and your studies. Promise you'll move on."

"Ellie," he breathed, brushing his nose past hers, "don't."

"Promise me."

She heard Max's voice ringing in her ears. *Run. You have to run. Promise me.*

She understood him at that moment now more than she ever had. The love she felt for Julian and Max's soul cut deeper than anything she had ever known before, and if tonight did end in failure, she needed to know that he would pick up the pieces of his life and continue. After all, he wasn't facing immortality without her. He was facing sixty, maybe seventy years. Plenty of time to meet someone else and fall in love. Start a family. Grow. Travel. Explore.

Julian hung his head.

She kissed him sweetly. "I need you to say it, Julian. If this doesn't work, you have to remember that I chose this, and that it was all I ever wanted. If it doesn't work, you still set me free."

He kissed her more deeply, his tongue pressing into her mouth and exploring her with desperation. His hand wandered down the length of her smooth, pale stomach, and settled between her thighs. He brushed against her wetness. She breathed in the scent of him—blood, sweat, and musk.

"Julian," she purred.

"I promise."

He pressed his fingers inside of her. She yielded to him and gave over control immediately. That was what tonight was all about, after all. Giving over control. Letting it all go. Succumbing to the inevitable.

He filled her up and kissed her at the same time, his tongue plunging into her mouth while his fingers drove into her core. She clung to him as her desperation mounted, and when she couldn't take it anymore, she hooked a leg over his hip and leveraged herself up and over, mounting him and pinning him on his back. Julian looked dazed. She must have moved a little too quickly for him.

When he gathered his wits, he gripped her thighs. She reached down between her legs and undid his pants. She pulled him free, stroked him, and rocked against his length. He pulled her down to him as she lifted herself, bracing herself with her hands against his chest, and lowered herself down on his length. He moaned beneath her. She sighed as he stretched her.

She rode him slowly, relishing every time he moved deep inside of her. Would sex feel different, too?

Beneath her, Julian turned his neck to the side, exposing his fluttering pulse and the tendons in his throat.

He didn't need to ask for what he wanted.

She dropped low, still riding him, and licked his skin before letting her fangs unsheathe. She nipped quickly and spared no blood. He gripped her thighs and held her down on him as she drank from him. As she did, Max's tangled memories came rushing to the surface, and like always, she saw through his eyes.

She saw herself in a meadow on a starry night. Pale-blue flowers appeared to glow under the light of the moon. Fireflies danced in the tall grass, and Max watched her as she danced naked amongst them.

Ellie knew this memory well. It was one she had wished she could relive so many times over the years. She'd known he'd been watching, and the dance was for him. He finally came to her in the grass, and they settled down amongst the dew. Hungry—always hungry—they'd spent no time getting each other ready. He dropped his pants and drove inside of her. She arched her back and lifted her hips.

While Julian clung to her and bucked beneath her, Max plunged into her in the memories, and Ellie succumbed to it all with a cry of pleasure when she came. Julian followed quickly after, and the memory went fuzzy.

When she came back to herself, she got the stars overhead confused for the fireflies in the memory.

She let out a dreamy sigh and snuggled into Julian, who wrapped an arm around her. She listened to his heart pound like thundering hooves across open fields.

"Whenever you're ready," he said after a long stretch of time.

"Not yet," she whispered. "At sunrise."

She lost track of time as they lay there. So many dreams and memories were supposed to be made on this very balcony—and many already had been. She and Max had stood in this very spot many times looking out at the surrounding lands, truly believing that would be their eternal view. Entertaining wistful thoughts, she talked about having children here and watching them grow up surrounded by the trees, hills, and small Spanish towns.

It would have been the perfect place to raise children.

She put a hand to her stomach.

She still felt that way, but with the Coven so close, she couldn't risk it. They would see Julian and her as traitors and stains upon the earth. And their child? Well, the child would be considered an abomination.

She had to protect what was hers, and she could only do that in New York.

"I want you to meet my family," Julian said as the sky began to lighten.

She curled up against him. How odd. Meeting his family. "Do you think they'll like me?"

"Of course," he said. She could hear the smile in his voice. "And you'll like them, I swear. Sometimes they can be a bit much, especially around the holidays, but hey, that's part of the whole human shtick, especially these days."

She rolled onto her stomach, rested her hands on his chest, and placed her chin upon her knuckles. "Tell me about them."

CHAPTER THIRTY-FOUR

As the dawn defeated the night, Julian held open the trapdoor for Ellie. She slipped back down into the lab and recalled the first time Max had ever shown it to her. It was the day he brought her to the manor for the first time. She was so young and naïve back then, and everything between them still felt so fresh and new even though they were in love. The Coven was in their blood back then. Sure, they were trying to distance themselves from the wickedness that had spread throughout the other vampires, but they were still family.

Especially her father, Aurelio.

Finding this manor had been a reprieve for them. Max had been the one to discover it, abandoned by humans. He brought her to it one night and revealed his plans to live here with her and build it anew to make it theirs.

They'd kept it a secret at first. Ellie had wanted it to be their safe place between all the patrolling they had to do at the time to protect the Coven from a rival group of vampires trying to move in on their territory. The enemy had slaughtered a nearby town to try to tip nearby hunters off to the Coven's location, and a full-blown war broke out. Aurelio would not stand for his lands to be taken from him. He would risk whatever it took to make sure the other vampires did not lay claim to the home the Coven had known for centuries.

Eleonor and Max hadn't wanted any part in that fight. Neither of them desired the kill the way the other vampires did, especially not the needless killing. Drinking blood to sustain one's own life could be justifiable, but killing families and every living breathing thing all over the territory?

That didn't sit well with either of them.

So, they'd made this their home. They weren't sure how long they could stay, or if they'd be in trouble when they were discovered, but things ended up working out well.

Until that night, of course.

Julian closed the trapdoor behind them, sealing them in his lab, and took Ellie's hand. He led her to the stone slab in the middle of the room and asked her to wait. She stood looking down at the cold piece of polished rock as he wet a rag in some sort of cleaning solution and used it to wipe Matteo's now-dried blood from the surface. He removed the chains and took his own pillow from his bed. He placed it on the top of the stone and offered her his hand to help her up.

She settled on her back on the slab and blinked up at the cobweb-filled rafters above.

Julian adjusted the pillow behind her head. She didn't bother telling him it was entirely unnecessary.

"Are you comfortable?" he asked.

She nodded.

He patted her wrist and went to his workstation, where she heard glass vials rattling around. She closed her eyes and listened. His heart was pounding so fast. His fingers trembled. His breathing was ragged and shallow.

"Julian," she said softly, "relax. Take a breath."

She listened as he inhaled through his nose and exhaled

through his mouth. He did this several times before he got a hold of his nerves and muttered a weak, "Thank you."

Ellie closed her eyes.

This is it.

This was the ending she never thought she would reach. Either she would die here, or all of her and Max's wildest dreams would come true. It felt natural to clasp her hands over her stomach.

Over the baby.

Even though breathing did her no good, she tried Julian's technique of inhaling through her nose and exhaling through her mouth. It felt foreign and odd.

Julian appeared beside her with a syringe in hand.

She looked at the clear liquid and bit down so hard on her cheek that she tasted blood.

"You have to come back to me after," Julian said, voice shaking.

She nodded. "I will."

"Are you ready?"

"Are you?"

He gave her an unconvincing smile that she suspected was meant to look daring. "Ready," he said.

The needle hovered over her vein.

She smiled up at him. "Go ahead. You won't hurt me. I believe in this."

He searched her eyes. "I love you."

"I love you, too." She used her free hand to reach across, take his hand, and help him guide the needle into her arm. She barely felt it. He drew a shaky breath. She could smell his fear. It permeated the room. She wished she could save him from it, but there was nothing she could do. Either this worked, or it didn't. She leveraged her finger over his on the back of the syringe. She knew he couldn't do it without her help. "I want this, Julian," she said, trying to lessen some of his burden. "You did not force it upon me. I chose it. I chose it three hundred years ago."

His eyes glistened. "What if it fails?"

"Then you will live on without me, and everything will be okay." Without waiting for his blessing, she pushed down on his thumb. The cure flooded her vein.

Julian gasped and grabbed her wrist. He squeezed reassuringly and watched as she made peace with her choice and relaxed upon the stone.

Suddenly, she was on fire. Every vein, muscle, nerve ending, capillary, and organ felt like it had been simultaneously lit on fire. It reminded her of the pyre and the night Max had burned. Had he felt like this? She held on to the scream that threatened to escape. She couldn't let Julian hear her cry out. It would hurt him more than the pain eating at her insides. She could bear it.

Julian called out to her, but he sounded so very far away, like she'd sailed away on a boat and left him at the dock. His voice faded until it sounded like nothing more than a memory, but the pain blazed on. Her ears rang and thundered, and it wasn't until she focused on that thundering that she realized what it was.

The sound of a beating heart.

Her chest tightened and ached.

She opened her mouth, longing to say something to Julian to spare him his worry, but the world went dark, and the walls closed in around her. She fought against the darkening corners of her vision for as long as she could. The last thing she saw was Julian's dark-blond hair as he hovered over her and tapped her cheeks, but she couldn't feel him.

All she could feel was cold.

She woke, and she was shivering. She could hear a heartbeat, but not her own, and she realized she was curled up in Julian's lap. He was wrapped around her, trying to give her warmth, and her cheek rested upon his chest. She murmured his name with a thick tongue and gripped the front of his shirt with trembling fingers. Her fist felt so weak—like she hadn't used it in decades.

"I'm here," he said softly, tightening his hold on her. "I'm here, and so are you. Ellie, can you feel it?"

She could hardly open her eyes. She felt so heavy and tired. "Feel what?"

"The sun."

At first, she didn't understand, but then she noticed the warmth upon her other cheek, not the one against his chest, and her shoulder and back. She focused on it, wondering how something could feel so wonderfully warm and she could still feel so terribly cold. Desperate, she opened her eyes and blinked against the glare of morning light.

Sunlight.

Ellie lifted a hand in the light of day. Sunlight streamed between her fingers, and her hand cast a shadow upon the grass beside them.

"It worked," Julian said, kissing the top of her head. "It worked, Ellie."

Everything sounded so quiet, like she was underwater. Birds chirped, and their song sounded lighter somehow. She could taste her own tongue and feel aches and pains that had never been there before. She felt nauseous, but even that was a nice feeling compared to the endless nothingness of the last few hundred years.

"Help me stand," she said.

Slowly, carefully, Julian slid out from under her. With one hand around her waist and another under her arm, he guided her up to her feet and held on to steady her. She faced the sun and let it kiss her cheeks. It felt even warmer up here off the damp, dewy grass. She breathed in deeply, smelling the fresh earth, the crisp morning air, and the smell of a fire somewhere in the distance.

Everything felt familiar and simultaneously foreign. It had been such a long time since she was human, and she wasn't the same girl she had been back then. She had lived too much life in between to be remotely the same person.

"How do you feel?" Julian asked.

It felt odd to stand beside him and not hear his heart beating.

"Like I'm alive," she whispered. Her throat felt raw. Had she screamed, even when she tried not to?

She stared out at the trees and the sun breaking over the tops of them. She had missed out on so much since she lost Max. How could she have forgotten how good the sun felt on her bare skin? She had half a mind to strip naked and bask in its warmth.

"Why not?" she muttered to herself.

Julian stood back when she pushed away and stripped out of her clothes.

"What are you doing?"

"I want to feel it," she said. "All of it. Everywhere."

She cast her clothes aside and reveled in the sunlight. It felt glorious upon her breasts and navel. She spread her arms out wide, daring the sun to burn her. What if this was temporary? What if she only had fleeting moments to feel this good?

Julian moved in behind her and drew her hair away from her neck to rest his chin on her shoulder. "We did it."

She turned in his arms. The sun warmed her back as she stood circled in his arms, hands pressed to his chest, breasts bare between them. He looked into her eyes. "You did it," she told him.

He bowed his head to kiss her.

For once, she didn't hear the rush of his blood or feel the need to drink him. She felt only the warm, pleasant buzz deep inside of her of desire and contentment mingled into one. She felt at peace.

Tears leaked down her cheeks.

Julian engulfed her in his arms when she started to sob, and she clung tightly to him.

"It's finally over," she exhaled.

EPILOGUE

Ellie held her coffee mug and gazed out the coffee shop window. It was raining, as it almost always did in New York, but sunlight broke through the clouds far overhead. It managed to peek between skyscrapers and hit the window right beside her, lighting up the beads of rainwater in the most magnificent way.

Julian returned to the table with a scone for each of them and some napkins.

He handed one plate to her.

She peered down at the cranberry and white chocolate scone before her with the little packet of butter on the plate. She set to work buttering and preparing it before taking a bite. Her eyes almost rolled back in her head.

"Good, right?" he asked.

"Almost better than sex."

He coughed on his scone and washed it down with a sip of his latte. "Ouch."

"I said *almost,*" she teased.

She and Julian had moved back to New York just over a week ago, and he was enjoying taking her to all of his favorite places across the expansive city. She had to admit, New York felt like a totally different place in the daylight. They'd been doing plenty of eating. As it turned out, most of his favorite places were restaurants of some sort. She'd discovered that she had a strong dislike for meat, so had been avoiding it. She preferred vegetarian dishes and didn't mind dairy, but steak and pork were not within the realm of possibilities of things she could eat. She wondered if that was because it reminded her of the texture of biting into human flesh.

It didn't matter. Either way, she wasn't interested in it.

Julian nodded down at her nearly-gone scone. "Do you want another one?"

She shook her head and patted her stomach. "I'm good."

She'd gained weight since coming home. She was no longer the thin, almost bony rack of a pale vampire she used to be. A full week of sun-chasing had left her nose and cheeks rosy. Her face was fuller and less gaunt. Her eyes were no longer sunken. The tendons in the backs of her hands didn't stand out so much. Her breasts were fuller, and her ass a little thicker, and she'd noticed some soft skin gathering around her tummy.

Julian chuckled and said it was a side effect of human food these days, but she knew better.

It was the baby growing inside of her.

She wasn't complaining. She loved her healthy complexion and changing body. She felt better for it. Not stronger, per se, but human, and after chasing that for such a long time, her reflection was a constant reminder that the past was where it finally belonged.

In the past.

"What do you want to do today before my classes?" Julian asked. "Go to the movies? Or a Broadway show? We could go to Central Park. You still haven't been there. We could ride a horse-drawn carriage. They won't be spooked by you anymore."

Ellie licked her lips and stared down into the depths of her tea latte. "Don't you think you'll get bored of all this stuff eventually?"

He frowned. "Bored? What? Never!"

She sighed. "It's just that you've done all these things dozens of times over. None of it is new or exciting for you. I worry that I'm going to, I don't know, wear on you with all this stuff."

He reached across the table and took her hand. It still surprised her when his touch was colder than hers. "Ellie, don't say such nonsense. Having you with me makes all these mundane things feel like Christmas morning."

She smiled. "Christmas morning, huh?"

He chuckled. "Come on, bring your tea with you. I have an idea of what we should do."

As she had been doing all week, she followed Max out into the city. He led her a few blocks down the street, stopping to point out more places for them to visit, like an authentic Spanish restaurant, a comedy lounge, and an arcade, which she had very little knowledge of what it was.

She felt unlike herself these days, but not in a bad way. She felt lucky and grateful, but also very vulnerable. She wasn't used to being wary of cars passing by or constantly being startled by things. Without her usual keen senses, people and loud noises were always catching her off guard. She didn't love that. Luckily, Julian was always by her side to remind her that she was okay.

He led her into a shop full of dresses and pretty clothes.

She'd never been able to do much shopping when she was a vampire because of the store hours and the conflicting sunlight. But now? She could go everywhere anytime she wanted. They sifted through the racks, and he pulled out cute items he said he wanted to see her in. She wasn't sure if he actually enjoyed this, but she desperately needed new clothes since she was running low and nothing fit her anymore.

Julian had helped her move out of her dingy basement suite

three days ago, even though she'd spent every waking minute and night with him since returning from Spain. He'd been appalled at how bleak the place was and hated thinking of her being there alone. She reminded him it had served a purpose. It protected her from the sun and humans when she needed it.

They brought her books to his library and added her collection to his. She felt content with her decision to never open another vampire book in her life. She was done with all that.

Julian ushered her into the fitting rooms and had her put on a show for him. She came out in jeans with black boots and long cardigans. He approved. She tried on scarves and winter coats for the New York winter—a strange necessity for her now—and he sent it all up to the register with one of the sales associates. She tried on dresses, skirts, sneakers, and shirts, and Julian insisted they buy everything she liked. She tried to talk him out of it, but he wouldn't take no for an answer, and they left with bags upon bags of things for her to wear.

She couldn't deny it gave her a little flutter of excitement. Not only did she have a new life, but she got to rediscover herself now. She no longer had to be the isolated, brooding, depressed, suicidal vampire she used to be. She could be the girl of her own making. A lover, a partner, a dancer, an adventurer—whatever she wanted, she could become. The possibilities were overwhelming, but Julian constantly reminded her she only had to worry about one step and one day at a time. The rest would come.

Somehow, she would have to find a way to thank him.

They returned home shortly before Julian had to get ready for class, and they stole half an hour in bed together, lying in each other's arms and making love. Sometimes she missed being able to bite him and see Max's memories, but she was making peace with that, too. That morning, she lay beneath him, half tangled up in white sheets as the sun shone through the window and he moved deep inside of her.

They made love every day and every night. She couldn't get enough of him and needed to feel as close to him as possible after everything they'd been through. He took care of her every time.

When they were done, he rolled out of bed and got dressed for school. She stayed where she was, still wrapped up and naked, and watched with hooded, lustful eyes as he pulled his pants on.

"When will you be home?" she asked.

"Nine o'clock," he said. "Late class tonight. But I can pick up dinner on the way home. Or we can order something?"

"Whatever you want to do."

He chuckled and moved to the bed to lean over and kiss her. "I want to do you."

She blushed. "Well, I'll be here waiting."

A few minutes later, he grabbed his bookbag and rushed out the door. The large house echoed with silence, and once she was sure he was gone, Ellie popped up out of bed and got herself dressed, too. She went downstairs, stepped outside, and locked up behind her before facing the rainy afternoon. She didn't bring an umbrella. She liked the rain.

She made the walk to the doctor's office where she'd managed to book an appointment a few days ago. The wait had killed her. She didn't quite know how to take care of herself yet as a human in a modern world, let alone a pregnant human. She needed medical advice, and she needed it quickly.

The walk was almost an hour and left her breathless and soaked from the rain. The receptionist in the clinic looked her over, gave her a warm and gracious smile, and fetched her a towel. Ellie felt grateful and foolish all at once. She dabbed herself dry and waited in the waiting room with other patients. It was eerily silent. She couldn't hear any of their heartbeats or smell their blood. If she listened carefully, she could hear their breathing, but there was nothing special about that.

Nothing special about her anymore, either.

How truly wonderful, she thought, smiling to herself.

The doctor called her in after waiting for twenty minutes, and they discussed her pregnancy. He confirmed she was pregnant, and very early along, and talked about the next steps she should expect. He wanted her to come back for another prenatal appointment in a month, and from there, they would set up her first ultrasound so she could see the baby.

Her heart raced, and it still felt so odd in her chest. She put her hand over it as if she could calm it. "We can't do an ultrasound sooner?" she asked.

He shook his head and adjusted his glasses on the bridge of his wide nose. "I'm afraid not. I understand how that can be stressful, and most mothers struggle with the wait for the first ultrasound because they want to make sure everything is okay. But we won't be able to detect anything yet. The fetus is still too small."

She nodded. Right. Too small, even though she'd been able to feel them a mere nine days ago. "Okay, what should I do in the meantime?"

He grinned. "Well, you want to focus on a healthy diet, if you can manage it. Do you have any pregnancy sickness so far?"

She shook her head.

"That's great. Focus on eating a balanced diet. You don't have to restrict yourself, but you want to make sure you're getting the proper nutrients to sustain yourself and the growing baby. I encourage movement and exercise with daily walks and twenty minutes of more vigorous exercise five days a week. I know it's a lot, especially if you're not feeling up to it, but it will benefit you in the long run. Oh, and try to manage your stress levels. Would you consider yourself a high-stress person?"

She thought about all the time that had passed and the

massive adjustment she was currently going through, and how Julian still didn't know about this baby, and how she'd booked this appointment specifically when she knew he'd be in school.

She shrugged.

The doctor gave her a knowing smile. "Well, try your best to find ways to release that stress. The walks and exercise will help. But you'll also want to lean on your support network. Your partner, your family, your friends."

"Of course," she murmured.

"We'll keep a close eye on things, but everything looks great to me so far, Ellie. Any other questions for me?"

Yes.

She shook her head.

Is my baby human?

Does it have fangs?

Is it going to consume me from the inside out?

Is this a sustainable pregnancy?

Should I be scared?

She held on to her racing thoughts and left the clinic, emerging back out into the rain once more.

Lighter, brighter thoughts followed the frightened ones. She wondered who this little soul would be one day. Would they be more like her, or more like their father?

Julian.

Would he resent her for keeping this a secret, or would he understand?

Her sweet, wonderful Julian. She knew deep down he would understand, even if he was disappointed that she hadn't felt comfortable confiding in him right away. This was a lot for her to process. After being alone for so long, she had suddenly been thrust into the most important role of all: motherhood. She worried she wouldn't be good enough, and that her years had made her too dark and twisty to do this well. On the flip side, she had wanted this literally longer than any other mother on the face of the planet. That had to count for something, didn't it?

She smiled and put her hand on her stomach as she walked. If she could weather the storm behind her, she could get through this, too. They all could, together.

She tipped her head to the sky as the clouds began to part and the sun dared to peek through.

"Hope dies last," she whispered to her baby, the universe, and her own soul that she was bringing back from the dead.

The End

ABOUT THE AUTHOR

E.B. Borbón is an emerging fiction author of speculative historical fiction, low fantasy and dark fiction. Fascinated with history growing up, his interest led to some early exposure to reading. He was drawn to cultures and customs that were different from his own. Finding beauty in things forgotten and abandoned, he started to write short stories about the people and places throughout history that fall between the well-known events. *The Fate of Eleonor* is E.B. Borbón's first published book

facebook.com/e.b.borbon
twitter.com/ebborbonauthor
instagram.com/e.b.borbon

Made in the USA
Monee, IL
16 December 2022

22138469R00144